THE BIG SKATE

SIERRA HOCKEY #3

ELISE FABER

THE BIG SKATE
BY ELISE FABER

Newsletter sign-up

THE BIG SKATE
Copyright © 2024 Elise Faber
Print ISBN-13: 978-1-63749-153-9
Ebook ISBN-13: 978-1-63749-152-2

SIERRA HOCKEY

CHAPTER ONE

Knox

"CLEAN AND JERK."

I feel my dick twitch, never able to hear the name of the exercise without my mind going somewhere dirty.

Especially when uttered by such a beautiful woman.

But since I'm currently hefting one hundred and fifty pounds over my head—the *jerk* part of the clean and jerk—I force myself to focus.

"Again," Ivy says, when I release the hold, allow the barbell to drop forward and settle onto the floor. "Smoother."

"You know," I mutter, exhaling and adjusting my grip, engaging my core, preparing myself to go again, "you can pair more than one word together and it forms something called sentences."

"Did that."

I glance over at her and raise a brow.

"Clean *and* jerk."

Watching her lush lips form those words, seeing the hint of humor in her deep brown eyes isn't helping my dick-twitching, but this is work—for me *and* her. And as a strength coach for the

NHL team, the Sierra (her) and a player for that same team (me), it's *important* work.

"That's *three* words," she says. Then jerks her chin toward the barbell. "Again."

Christ.

She's beautiful and smart and hardworking.

And *diligent.*

I grind my teeth together, but I exhale and heft the bar up to my shoulders then grunt as I extend it fully overhead and end up in a split stance.

My quads are screaming, along with my hamstrings and glutes, my core and biceps and triceps.

So yeah, pretty much my entire body is on fire.

That's what happens with Ivy's training. It's not even that the weight is all that heavy or that the reps—three sets of eight—are overwhelming. It's that she curates a careful list of exercises to target exactly where we need strengthening.

It's the middle of the season, a time that's normally reserved for maintaining strength and nursing the injuries that come from playing such a physical and brutal sport as hockey, but we have almost a week off and…

Ivy's decided that we need targeting.

Fun. Fun.

And normally, it *is*. I enjoy working out, am proud of my body and the strength I've worked so hard for. But lately…

It began as an itch between my shoulder blades, a restlessness in my hands, in my feet and fingers and toes. It crept into my sleep and stole my rest. Sucked the joy out of shit that I normally love and—

Two of my closest friends fell in love—one of them with my sister, and the other with her best friend, who may as well be my surrogate sister.

My agitation isn't typical male bullshit, my protective instincts triggered by them being old enough to have sex with someone.

Okay, so that's not my favorite.

But...I pushed them together, Lake and Nova, Ella and Riggs. Leo and Jolie, I can't take responsibility for, but they're in just as deep as the other two couples.

So, it's not protectiveness or even that our nights out carousing or picking up chicks don't happen any longer. They don't, of course—the guys are far more likely to want to hang out with their women than without them and, swear to fuck, I haven't seen either of them look at another member of the opposite sex since they fell in love. But I still hang with them, and not just at hockey. We have dinners and Game Nights and spend many an evening at the local watering hole, drinking beer and the occasional honey rosemary Moscow mule.

So, I still see my friends regularly. And I see my sister, Ella, and the woman I consider one, Nova, just as often.

Plus, the season is going well—I'm putting up points, making good plays.

My life is great.

Except for the fucking itch between my shoulder blades.

"Again," Ivy orders.

"Yup," I grunt.

"Three more."

"Yup." Another grunt.

"To eight."

"Yup," I grit out, lowering the bar and repeating the movement with, yup, another grunt. "Of that I am aware."

"Great," she mutters, watching me complete another rep before she turns and moves to Riggs, correcting the angle of his wrists in his overhead press.

By the time I finish my last reps and she's made a circle of the room, checking in with all of us who are here, putting in our hours in the weight room, I've finished my set as well as the last exercise on my list (fucking Bulgarian split squats).

"Time to stretch and hydrate," she orders.

"A full sentence?" I feign shock. "Wow."

She rolls her eyes and picks up one of the shakes the team nutritionist makes for us—taking our particular needs and preferences into account—passing it over. "Hydrate," she says again. "Stretch."

And then she's off, moving over to Lake, who's nursing a sore shoulder, helping him through a series of stretches and some special one-on-one time with a tiny ball that's great at targeting knots in muscles, but also terrible...because it's great at targeting those knots.

Better him than me, I know, chugging down my shake and making quick work of my assigned stretches.

I leave our captain sweating—not from the workout so much as the targeting of that little ball—and head to the showers, determined to scrub at the space between my shoulders until the itch goes away.

Or maybe blast it off with scorching hot water.

Unfortunately, the shower doesn't erase the sensation and by the time I'm driving home, I'm exhausted but still squirmy. I know I won't be able to sleep.

A-fucking-gain.

I still go through the motions anyway.

Healthy dinner with lots of lean protein, complex carbs, and plenty of veggies.

Turning off screens an hour before bed.

Reading a dry, historical non-fiction, hoping that I'll pass out before I reach the next chapter.

Alas...it's not to be.

I trudge through one chapter. Then another. And another. And—

Sighing, I toss my book to the side, throw back the blankets, and get dressed.

If reading isn't going to do the trick then I'll run myself into exhaustion and hope that my brain finally gets the memo.

Unfortunately, it's not that easy. My brain won't quiet all through the first mile and my body perks up, a rush of adrenaline and endorphins from the exercise filling my system. I'm *more* awake. And that doesn't change through the second mile.

Or the third.

By the time I'm on my fourth, I'm still not tiring, but I slow my pace anyway because…

"What the—?"

I skid to a halt, heart skipping a beat when I catch the soft whimper at the edge of my hearing. Cursing quietly, I hurry to the edge of the quiet road, the hillside still covered with snow. It's far too cold for anyone to be out here and I search the shadows for the source of the sound.

When I find it, I curse again.

A tiny dog is wrapped in a dirty blanket, its hair plastered to its head, its eyes filled with pain…

And it doesn't take long to recognize why—

The poor thing's leg isn't pointed the right direction.

"Fuck," I mutter, quickly stooping down.

The pup growls at me, and I slow my movements.

"Easy, buddy," I murmur, carefully shifting closer. "I'm not going to hurt you."

Another growl, but with less enthusiasm this time around, so I take it as my cue to move a little closer.

"Damn," I whisper, mentally weighing my options. I don't want to move him, but I also can't leave him here, out in the cold. And I'm not all that far from home. "Okay, bud," I say in a gentle tone, careful to keep my movements slow and easy, my voice calm, "I'm going to get you some help, but that means I need to pick you up." I slip one hand beneath his good leg. "Unfortunately, that means this may hurt a little." Using my forearm, I do my best to support the injury as I slide my other hand beneath him and lift.

Slowly.

Easily.

He growls, but he doesn't bite me as I cradle him against my chest.

"There," I whisper, "that's not so bad, right?"

A soft whimper has me feeling like shit, but I don't stop. He's shivering and hurting, and I need to get him help.

When I get to my house, I earn another growl and cause another whimper and feel like shit again, but I manage to get the garage door open and the pup into the back of my car. It only takes a moment to snag my keys and wallet from the house, to look up the address for the emergency vet on my phone.

Then I'm carefully navigating down my driveway and turning out onto the dark road.

CHAPTER TWO

Ivy

"Look, Mom!"

I grit my teeth together, bite back my sigh.

She loves me. She wants to spend time with me. And...I love her. Love being a mom. Love our home that we've made in the Tahoe basin.

There's peace here, and well-paying work.

It's just that I really don't want to look at the twentieth drawing that my daughter, Evie, has made since I picked her up from school.

I admire her dedication and her neatness, just...not her artistic abilities.

Especially not when I'm flat on my back, crammed between the fridge and the tiny space behind it, trying to fix the leak in the ice maker.

"*Mom!*"

"Just a second, honey," I say, stretching a little further, trying to get the wrench positioned correctly so I can tighten the nut that's the cause of all my problems—or at least the ones that mean I keep coming home to find a puddle spreading out from beneath the fridge.

"But Mom," she whines. "This one is really good. It's has me and Rylie"—her best friend at school—"and you."

The wrench slips and the water starts coming faster. I grit my teeth together. "Neat, honey."

"And we're all making a snowman."

"Cool, baby." I reposition the wrench, manage to tighten the screw enough that the water slows down.

Finally.

I go again, tighten it further, relief coursing through me as the flow turns into a drip then turns into *not* a leak.

"Thank you, sweet baby Jesus," I whisper, my eyes flying to the ceiling and a sigh of relief sliding through me.

I still have a mess to clean up, but…progress.

"And there's a carrot nose and sticks for arms and coal buttons, all like the song!"

I start wriggling backward, making a mental note to clean back here before I return the fridge to its proper position…and before I start creating my own ecosystem behind it. "No top hat?" I ask as I shift to my knees and resist the urge to scrub my damp, dust-covered hands over my face.

"Oh!" she says, clutching the paper, drawing side in, to her chest. "*That's* what I forgot!"

She spins on her heel, her long red braids swinging behind her —my girl loves her braids, no matter how messy my attempts turn out—and she runs back into the living room, presumably to add that top hat to her drawing. Free for the moment, I take the chance to wash my hands, attempt to fix my own braid she insisted I corral my hair in to (the bane of my existence, my daughter learning what braids are), and then turn back to what I was doing before I noticed water seeping out beneath the fridge—

Laundry.

Oh, the life of a single mom.

It's so much fun.

"Look, Mom!"

I glance up from the socks I'm matching and plaster the right kind of expression on my face—interested, focused, proper attentive mama. I *ooh* and *aah* over the neatness and the colors, compliment her slightly better than stick figures...and then I repeat the process with a half-dozen others she brings my way for inspection as I fold.

I finish the laundry, clear out the sink—why does it always seem to be filled with dirty dishes? And then it's time for both of us to have a snack and for my little Evie to get into her karate uniform.

More Mom Duties.

I snag my computer and Evie's bag then hustle us both out to the car, intending on doing some multitasking during Evie's class.

Player programs to review, modifications to make, and doing some planning for the private clients that I see on the side—something that's grown much smaller in number now that I work full-time with the team, but something I'm also not willing to give up.

And not just because of the extra money my long-time clients bring in.

I enjoy working with them, supporting the progress they've made over the years—getting stronger, managing pain, claiming back mobility.

And also...

Fall-back plan.

It's always important to have a fallback plan.

The drive to the karate studio isn't long, but I can't help sighing in pleasure as we wind through the roads. There's something about the pine trees and the snow, even the gray sky overhead. Safe and hidden, our own private space—at least until we get into the busy downtown area and I spend a solid five minutes circling the karate studio's parking lot for a spot.

Eventually, I squeeze my car into one that's not terribly far from the studio, grab our stuff, and get settled inside.

In between watching my six-year-old practice her kicks and punches (and once, very impressively, her take-down skills when her instructor taught her a sweep), I'm working on my files.

Even with all of that going on, though, I'm still hyper aware of a man coming into the studio partway through class.

Hyper aware because he sits directly next to me.

And there aren't any other parents watching.

So...to be in the seat next to me?

Yeah, not loving that.

I may work with a full roster of gorgeous hockey players, but I'm sure as fuck not in the market for a man. I've made my own way for far too long to let some asshole with an itch to scratch into my life.

I don't do one-night stands.

And I don't expose my daughter to men who'll walk away.

And, let's face it, they always do.

Plus, I don't eat where I shit—and fucking one of the parents from my daughter's karate class...

Well, I think that's got to be pretty close to the precise definition of exactly that.

So, I do my best to stay focused on what's important—my work and my daughter.

Alas, the man doesn't take the nonverbal hint (and really, do they ever?) because he follows Evie and I out of the studio, his son by his side.

"Excuse me?"

I clench my jaw, but I turn and force a smile. "Yes? Can I help you?"

He's handsome, this man. In good shape and with all his hair and he has kind eyes, but I don't let that sway me—*can't* let it sway me. "Hey, you're Evie's mom, right?"

I nod, glance down at my daughter. "Yup. I'm Ivy." A nod to his son. "And you belong to Max?"

A grin. "I sure do." He extends his hand, and I shake it. "Tom."

"Hi, Tom."

We spend a few minutes chatting about the instructors and how much fun the kids are having in class before the moment I've been dreading happens. "You know," he begins. "I was wondering if you might be interested in going out—"

Dammit.

I flick my stare to Evie again, see the rapt focus she's displaying for this conversation, and...know that I have to nip this in the bud.

This usually doesn't end well and I don't want her exposed to a shitshow.

I dig into my pocket, pull out my keys, and pass them over to her. "Why don't you get into the car, honey?"

Her nose wrinkles, and I think she'll argue—not wanting to miss out on the action—but then her gaze connects with Max and something passes between them.

Something that gives me a sinking sensation.

Because...that *something* is plotting.

Damn. It's worse than I thought.

"Okay, Mom!" she chirps, running over to the car. I watch her get in, make sure she closes the door, and when I turn back to my special brand of hell, it's to see Max having done the same (albeit getting into his own car) and Tom still standing there looking hopeful.

Double damn.

"Look," I say and immediately his expression falls. I feel like shit, but I have to keep pushing on, have to end this before it gets worse. "You seem really nice, and Max is a gem, but I'm not interested in dating anyone right now."

"Max said that Evie said—"

"No," I interrupt.

Just...*no.*

It's simpler that way.

Of course, the true assholes don't always take no for an answer.

Thankfully, Tom proves different—at least on this front.

He studies me for a second. Then he sighs and his mouth ticks up. "Been burned, huh?"

Relief slides through me because...he's not going to make this hard.

"Too many times to count," I admit.

"I'm sorry about that." He reaches out as though to touch my arm, but before I can step back, he drops his hand to his side. "Right." A tilt of his head to the studio. "We'll see you around."

I nod. "I—" I clear my throat. "Thank you for the thought."

"You're welcome."

We stand there awkwardly for a second before I put us both out of our misery by joining Evie in the car.

"Did you say yes?" she asks before the door even slams shut.

I stifle a sigh. "Honey, I—"

"You said no," she mutters and when I flick my gaze to the rear-view mirror, checking that she's buckled in, I see she's scowling.

Sigh.

"I said no, sweetheart," I agree. "Tom seems nice, and I know Max is your friend, but I'm perfectly happy with my life right now."

Evie scowls. "But what about when I get married and move out?"

God help me.

"Well, maybe then I'll be lonely and want to look for someone." I turn around now, holding her eyes so she knows this is one of those times that I mean business. "But, right now, I'm not interested in dating anyone, okay?"

She sighs and flops back in her booster seat, mutiny in every line of her being.

"I'm never going to have a dad, am I?"

CHAPTER THREE

Knox

"So HE IS ACTUALLY A HER," the vet, Dr. Karlson, says as she ushers me into the back room of the emergency veterinarian facility.

There are floor-to-ceiling kennels, most of them empty, but a few of them house cats and dogs who look like they've had better days.

Including the little guy I scooped up from the side of the road.

Or girl, apparently.

"Now that we've got her cleaned up we have a better idea of what her injuries are." She stops and bends down next to a crate, and I see him—*her*.

God, she's even more of a pathetic sight than when I first spotted her on the side of the road.

Her back right leg is wrapped in a pink cast and the parts of her that aren't covered in blankets are dotted with shaved patches of fur. I wince at the array of abrasions and cuts, some deep enough that they obviously required sutures.

Damn. Poor thing

"—and they're not good."

My heart squeezes and I tear my gaze from the pup, glance over at the doc. "Not good in what way?"

"Her gums are pale, and her tummy is bloated. Her temperature is still far too low. Likely there's some internal damage that didn't show up on our original scans." She shakes her head. "She needs more tests and, likely, surgery."

I glance at the tiny thing and find her eyes locked on me.

She looks pathetic.

Tiny and pathetic and miserable.

And my heart squeezes again.

"Can you fix her?" I ask softly.

There's a long moment of quiet and then the vet exhales. "I can try." A beat. "But it won't be cheap."

"Whatever it costs," I tell her. "I'll pay it."

Dr. Karlson is quiet for a minute, but I don't miss the glimmer of approval in her eyes before she nods. It makes me...

Feel things I shouldn't.

But I knew from the moment I heard that whimper I wasn't walking away.

"Okay," she says, brushing her palms on her thighs and straightening. "You can swipe a card with the receptionist before you leave. We'll draw up an estimate and take a deposit."

I wave a hand at that. I could give her cash right now if she needed it. More importantly—

"You'll do your best to save her?"

A nod. "Yes, Mr. Adler. I'll do my best to save her." She tilts her head to the door we walked through a couple of minutes ago. "Why don't you wait out front while the nurse draws up the paperwork and I'll get started on back here."

"Ok—"

But I don't even finish the word before she's turning away, already down to business. "Tiff, Rachel," she calls. "You're both with me. Ronnie, can you work on that estimate and payment for Mr. Adler?"

There are more clipped out orders, all accompanying a flurry of activity as I move back out to the front of the vet office.

It's quiet, and the wait is interminably long.

But eventually they come out with an estimate and the news that the pup is in surgery.

I sign away on the eye-wateringly expensive paperwork and even though they say I can go home and they'll call me, I wait.

And *wait*.

Until the dawn sunlight begins creeping into the windows.

Until the waiting room begins to be filled with different patients—these of the far less emergent variety.

I sit through a shift change and dawn turning to morning and I've pretty much lost all hope when the doors to the back swing open and I see Dr. Karlson come out.

She looks exhausted and pale, but…

She's smiling.

And my heart squeezes so hard that it feels as though I may pass out.

"She's stable" are her first words.

The relief is so intense that my head spins. It makes no sense. The dog's not even mine, and it's not like I can keep her. I'm on the road for half the fucking year.

"Really?" I rasp.

She nods. "Really. She'll need to be in here for the next week or so, at the very least, but I'll keep you posted so you can come by and visit."

I nod. "I can visit but I can't—"

Only before I finish that, the door to the vet swings open and a man runs inside, holding a huge German shepherd in his arms. Blood stains its sides and Dr. Karlson takes one look at him before running over.

I don't hold it against her—of course I don't.

The dog is in rough shape, and it needs her.

But it does take away the opportunity for me to make it clear that I can't keep the little pup.

"Let's get some help out here!" she calls.

And then everyone's moving at once—a stretcher is brought out, the pup is taken into the back, information taken, and…

I'm in the way.

And the pup is stable.

And fatigue is gnawing at my bones.

They have my number—both for my cell and my credit card. They'll be in touch.

So, I go home.

I shower and collapse into my bed, my back and shoulders aching from sitting in the unforgiving reception chair for hours.

Thankfully, my exhaustion is louder.

And it doesn't take long for me to slip off into sleep.

But it also doesn't escape me that I make sure to turn my phone on full volume before I do.

———

"SHOOT!"

I hold the puck on my stick, the shouted command from the stands almost making me smile.

If I wasn't in the middle of a game, in the middle of a power play, trying my best to not fuck up against the surprisingly challenging opponent, the Grizzlies, I might have.

But the league's newest expansion team made some key trades in the off-season, and now they have a formidable roster that makes them dangerous to play against.

"SHOOT!"

I ignore that—as I always do—and keep the puck on my blade as I cross over the top of the circles, trying to draw one of the assholes from the other team near enough to me that one of my teammates will be open. Of course that means I earn a slash to the hands, a shove to the back, and shoulder-to-shoulder contact that nearly knocks me off my skates for my trouble.

But it also buys me enough time to make a play—and Lake enough space to skate hard to the net.

Riggs is right behind him, streaking down from his position at the blue line, stick down, ready for me to pass.

So I do.

I flick the puck, and it flies toward Riggs, landing just before his stick. He corrals it without issue—and without stopping, moving hard to the goal.

He winds up, and it seems as though everyone holds their breath, waiting for his wicked slap shot.

But he doesn't follow through—or not with the ripper of a shot.

Instead, he slides the puck to the left...

And right onto Lake's stick.

The net is wide open, but it wouldn't matter if it wasn't.

Because Lake Jordan doesn't miss when he's that close to the goal.

Almost faster than my eyes can track, the puck is off his stick and flying into the back of the net.

The red light goes.

The crowd explodes.

And that goal is what sends us straight into winning the game and earning those two points in the standings.

When I get off the ice, finish my post-game interviews, cool down, and then, finally, shower, I see a text from the vet's office on my phone.

Or, I guess, a text from Dr. Karlson herself.

"Shit." My heart sinks and I hurry to open the message.

And then it sinks another few inches.

Because I know I'm fucked.

> She misses you. Come and visit tomorrow around ten.

CHAPTER FOUR

Ivy

"Good," I say watching as Storm squats with the barbell held securely over his shoulders.

A younger forward, who's newer to the league, he's still working on building his strength.

His speed is incredible. His agility and hockey smarts are off the charts.

But his strength isn't quite here yet.

He has the height, but his body is still that of a boy transitioning into manhood.

No worries, though, I'll have him whipped into shape in no time.

He grunts quietly as he finishes the last rep, and I pat him on the shoulder after he's reracked the barbell. "Nice work."

A nod.

"The meal plan still working for you?"

He nods again, but there's something in his eyes that has me wrapping my hand around his upper arm and tugging him away from where the rest of the team is working.

"What is it?" I ask, dropping my hand and fixing him in

place with my best Mom Stare (and really, it's also my best Get My Hockey Players to Behave Stare).

"The plan's fine," he says quickly, eyes sliding from mine. "I mean, vegetables aren't my favorite but the recipes you shared are better and the meal prep service makes it easy."

I pause, waiting to see if he's going to say anything else—or tell me what's really bothering him—and when he doesn't, I lift an eyebrow and wait for a bit longer.

He's young and my Get Hockey Players to Behave Stare is really good, so it doesn't take him much longer to cave.

"I'm hungry."

The words are so far away from what I expected him to say—which was anything from not liking the diet and needing more variety, to craving his favorite type of junk food, to being really, *really* freaking tired of greens and rice and chicken—that I stand there for a moment, gaping at him.

"You're *hungry?*"

His cheeks go just the slightest bit pink and his, no pun intended, storm cloud gray eyes darken. "Yeah," he mutters.

Thankfully that's all it takes for me to snap out of my shock. "Then we add more calories," I say.

Those eyes widen. "What?"

"If you're hungry," I tell him, snagging my laptop and bringing it back over to him, "then we add more calories. You're working hard and trying to build muscle, so you need fuel, bud. And"—I lean in, dropping my voice—"you don't need to restrict yourself or wait for me to okay it. Just eat and we'll figure out the best way to adapt what your body needs to your plan. It doesn't have to be perfect, remember? We're thinking long term here, yeah?"

"Yeah," he whispers.

"Add in what you need and let's track for the next week anything that isn't listed on the plan." I type a few notes into my laptop. "And then we'll check in and see where we are. That work for you?"

Another "Yeah."

Smiling, I pat him on the shoulder. "Good." A tilt of my head back to his loaded barbell. "Then do one more set, put your weights away, and you're done for the day."

"Got it," he says, snagging his water bottle and going back to the barbell in question. But he pauses before he lifts it. "Ivy?"

"Yeah?"

"Thanks."

I exhale quietly, feel it in my soul.

Storm's one of the good ones.

"Anytime," I tell him.

He nods, gets back to work.

I keep an eye on him as he finishes that last set, and then I make my rounds, checking in on all the guys. We're all wrapping up here—all except Knox, who came in late, looking haggard with dark circles beneath his eyes.

He still has half his workout left, and he's moving slower than normal, lifting lighter than normal, doing fewer reps than normal.

He's been like this for a couple of days now, and while I might have once chalked one night up to him tying one on and staying out too late—the Adlers love to party—three nights in a row is unusual for him.

If it was another player—one who didn't make my skin crawl with sensation, who didn't set my nerves on fire, who didn't shoot my awareness of him into the stratosphere—I would be over there, using my Get Hockey Players to Behave Stare and ferreting out all the secrets, like I had with Storm.

But Knox isn't Storm.

He's far more dangerous—at least to me.

So, I do my requisite checks, make sure he's lifting safely, that he's being careful.

As always, that's not an issue.

His body is a work of art, and though I've played a small role in fine-tuning things, the effort has all come from him.

Late nights. Early mornings. Extra workouts. Following the meal plan to a tee (though the last is likely because I've built in a certain amount of nights out and honey rosemary Moscow mules into his calorie count).

He's put in the work.

Which is why it's so concerning to see him like this.

I waffle between letting it go and broaching the topic with him as I make my final rounds, and I'm girding my loins—because I know for as much as I'm delaying it, I need to approach to the grumpy hockey player—when I sense movement in the doorway.

Coach is standing there.

Travis Hiller is smart, talented, and…

A total asshole.

He has been from the moment I began working with the Sierra, and he has one of those personalities that assures me he'll continue being one long after either of us leaves.

"My office. Now."

I open my mouth, ready to tell him that we're not done here, but one look at his face tells me that's both a fight I won't win and a fight I don't want to start.

Who's about to be on the other end of a reaming that's only going to get worse if that shit's delayed?

This girl.

Awesome.

I bite back the words and make a mental note to check in on Knox later. It'll be better to tear the Band-aid off with Hiller now, to get through the word vomit, and then get back to it.

"Move it," he bellows, eyes fixing on mine, giving me absolutely no opening to avoid this, and I grind my teeth together.

My stomach churns—it's like that scene outside the karate studio, only Hiller isn't going to reveal himself as a good guy.

I already *know* he's awful.

But I'm made of steel.

I won't wither just because some asshole wants to have a go at me.

I lift my chin.

"Move it," he snaps before I can tell him that I'm fucking busy, you know, doing my fucking *job*, "*Now*." And then he's gone, the door slamming behind him.

Ugh.

I snag my computer, tell the stragglers to be careful as they finish up, to not forget to hydrate and stretch before they hit the showers, then I start to slip from the room.

"Ivy?"

I turn to see Lake staring at me, concern obvious on his face. "Yeah?"

"You good?"

I want to go to that office like I want another freaking hole in my head, but I've survived far worse than anything that Travis Hiller can dish out. Even so, that Lake is asking at all means a lot. He's softened so much since he fell in love with Nova.

"I'm good," I murmur. "But thanks."

He nods, expression telling me that he doesn't particularly like my answer. Considering that he's been on the receiving end of plenty of Hiller's lectures, that's not exactly a surprise.

I touch his shoulder. "Promise," I add.

"If that changes…"

Okay, so not *all* men are bad.

Yes, logically, I knew this before.

It's just…the ones I pick who are awful.

Stifling a groan as I shut off that train of thought—I need to be firing on all cylinders to deal with Hiller—I tuck my computer under my arm when my stare collides with Knox's in the mirror.

My lungs tighten. My pussy flutters. My—

More things to shove down and ignore.

His eyes blaze into mine for a long moment, a sharp current

of awareness running between us, before I manage to tear myself away.

Enough.

I slip out into the hall, walk to the head coach's office, and then I knock.

"Come in."

A breath to steel myself before I turn the handle, push inside, and find him sitting behind his desk.

"Have a seat, Ivy," he says, tone far softer than before, far calmer, the abrupt shift in his mood almost giving me whiplash.

I sit in the chair in front of his desk, wary gaze focused on him, braced for whatever the hell is about to happen.

I know it's not going to be anything good.

It's *never* anything good.

But I'm still not prepared.

His chair rolls back as he stands, hitting the wall with a *thunk* as he rounds the large, wooden desk and steps between it...

And the chair he ordered me to sit in.

I lean back as he crouches down.

I tense as his hands settle on my knees.

But nothing's worse than what happens to me when he begins to speak.

CHAPTER FIVE

Knox

I NAMED THE FUCKING DOG.

And worse, I named her Winter.

God, I'm an idiot and not even a creative one.

I visited the vet against my better judgement and—

I'm an idiot *and* a sucker.

She's still weak and healing from her surgery, being pumped full of round the clock antibiotics, but...

She wagged her tail today.

When I walked into the back room of the vet's office this morning to sit next to her kennel, give her scratches, and keep her company—after staying far too late last night doing the same —her fluffy little tail had wagged.

At the sight of *me*.

And so, even though I'd intended to tell Dr. Karlson that I'd pay the expenses, but they needed to find a home for Winter...

The words hadn't come last night.

Or this morning.

Or through my text messages.

Winter saw me, and wagged her tail.

I'm so totally fucked.

And exhausted.

And I can't fucking sleep—I'm either worried about a fucking fluffball or I'm dreaming about a gorgeous redhead who can't fucking stand the sight of me.

Or my voice.

Or my jokes.

Or, well, *anything* about me, really.

So, it's fear that I'm going to lose a dog I shouldn't be thinking about keeping—and yeah, yeah, I know it's far more than *thinking* at this point, as I've already ordered bowls and food, beds and toys and have an appointment to meet with a dog sitter for the team's away games. The ordering I did when I woke up in the middle of the night, dreaming about being inside Ivy's tight little cunt and knowing that it's never going to happen. The scheduling was after my morning visit with Winter.

Fucking losing it.

Sleep is—

Problematic to say the least, and I know I have to find a way to fix it.

I can't go on like this.

Can't keep wanting Ivy.

Can't keep Winter—

"Fuck," I grit, knowing that for all the *can'ts,* Winter has become something that's nonnegotiable.

She's mine.

I'm keeping her.

No use pretending otherwise at this point.

She's a fighter, and I'm not going to take a chance that someone may not look after her as well as they should.

"Jesus, Adler," I grunt, shoving the thoughts out of my brain and continuing through my workout. It's a tough one—Ivy's plan to fine tune every inch of my body playing nicely with my own preferred methods of working out. Well, it's less *nice* and more brutal, but the rest of my workouts this week will be focused on recovery, so getting my ass kicked is what I need today.

Especially, if it'll help me finally be exhausted enough to sleep.

I power through the set, adding a few pounds here and there, an extra set in an exercise, another movement when the inspiration strikes.

I need to keep moving. Need to tire my body so my mind follows.

Need to—

"You never learn, do you?"

I still at the sound of Ivy's voice then straighten with a grunt, my legs on fire—

Hell, at this point, my entire *body* is on fire.

But I don't stop moving.

I *can't* stop.

If I stop, the voices get too loud and—

The dumbbells are ripped out of my hands, and I whip around to face her, growling, "What the fuck?"

Ivy drops them onto the rack and whirls around to face me. "The workout ended two hours ago."

God, she's beautiful.

Even when she glowers at me.

Even when there are shadows in her eyes that call to my soul to don some fucking armor and mount a white steed and ride to the rescue.

Not that she'll ever let that happen.

Not that *I* will.

Work hard. Cling to exhaustion. Sleep. *Finally* sleep.

I move to the squat rack, but she steps in front of me, blocking my path.

I shrug in silent answer then move to the bike. If she won't let me do weights then I'll just do more cardio until I hit the point of no return and make my way home.

I sit down, start to clip in, and—

She yanks the plug out of the wall. "That's *enough*," she grits out.

Fucking women.

Fucking *woman*.

I stand up, avoiding the weights, the bike, *and* the resistance bands—because she'll probably just take those away too, or try to, anyway—and make my way to the pull-up bar, jumping with a grunt (and significant burning in my quads).

Ignoring the pain, I start driving.

One. Two. Three—

A hand on my leg, yanking down, nearly succeeding in dislodging me.

"Get a fucking clue, lioness," I snap, shaking her off and continuing. "I'm not stopping."

"Ugh!" She tosses up her hands, shakes her head. "Fine. You want to fuck up your body by pushing it too hard? Whatever. But just remember that your team needs you for the playoffs, so if you injure yourself like an idiot because you don't know when to quit, that's on *you*."

Rant complete, she marches away, giving me a glimpse of those seriously toned legs, that lush ass.

Fucking sexy as shit.

There's a reason she's in my dreams every fucking night.

Ignoring the bolt of lust as I always do—or as I've done since she made it very clear she wasn't interested, I keep going.

Four. Five. Six—

She's reached the door now, but...pauses.

Seven. Eight. Nine—

No, not *pauses*. She's jiggling the handle and...

Ten.

I jump down, swipe my arm over my forehead and move over to her. "What's the matter?"

She jerks away from me when I get close then scowls up at me. "The door's locked."

"It's *never* locked."

"You think I don't know how to turn a handle, *along* with knowing nothing about how to do my job?" she grinds out.

I wince. "I didn't say that."

"Maybe not in so many words," she mutters.

And…that's hurt in her eyes.

Fuck.

"Ivy."

She steps back, mask firmly in place. "Never mind." She nods at the knob. "Weren't you about to mansplain how to open a door for me?"

"Lioness—"

She waves a hand at the door. "Nope. Let's see it, hotshot. Turn that handle because, clearly, this little lady"—now she waves that hand at herself—"can't figure out something *oh, so complicated.*"

Sighing, but knowing I won't get any further, certainly not now that I've pissed her off, I bite back my response and reach for the handle.

It turns beneath my fingers, and I look over to see the fury on her face when she realizes that she really *was* struggling to open a door—

But that's quickly replaced with dismay.

Because…

The knob comes off in my hand.

Gaping, I stare at the door, at the empty spot where the handle had once been. Then look back at her.

"What the fuck?" she breathes, beautiful brown eyes wide.

"I—"

She pushes by me to shove at the door.

It doesn't budge.

Then she scrabbles at the metal pieces of the lock, trying to get them to engage—

But they don't move either.

Slowly, she turns to face me, horror on her face.

Because…

We're trapped.

CHAPTER SIX

Ivy

THIS IS MY NIGHTMARE.

I've just spent the better part of the last hour trapped with the asshole head coach, Travis Hiller, listening to him tear apart my performance...and avoiding—

I shudder, shove the tangle of emotions down.

I can't think about pointed innuendos and wandering hands and having to slide my chair back inch by inch until it was almost at his office door so he couldn't touch me.

Right now, I have bigger problems to deal with.

Namely, the fact that I'm in a room with Knox Adler...

And the fucking doorknob has just come off in his hand.

I yank it away from him. "What the fuck did you just do?" Heart pounding, I try to fit it back into place. If I can just get the pieces to align then I can twist the handle and we'll be out of here.

But no matter which way I turn it or how hard I push it into the hole, the metal knob won't stay in place.

And the door sure as shit won't open.

Exhaling in defeat, I grind my back teeth together and resist the urge to pound my head against the door.

This is fine.

Everything is fine.

Meanwhile, I'm stuck in here with—

"Are you okay?"

Fucking *Knox*.

His voice slides like silk down my spine, dipping between my legs sending such a war of emotions through me that I have to actually lock my knees to keep upright.

Dumb. So fucking *dumb*.

"I'm fine," I snap. "Except for the fact that we're stuck in here."

I have things to do.

People to get far the fuck away from.

Memories to shove down and forget about.

"It's not a big deal," he says, because nothing is *ever* a big deal to him. *Nothing* fazes him. Not women. Not hockey. Not hard as hell workouts. And not, apparently, being locked in a room with a woman who hates him.

Or one who's trying to, anyway.

"I'll just call security," he goes on, "and they'll call maintenance, and we'll be out of here in a jiff."

"A j-jiff?"

The incongruity of hearing a big, sexy hockey player say *in a jiff* means that I'm slow to process him walking over to his duffle bag that's shoved into the corner of the room.

But I don't miss him bending over because...

Ho, mama.

That ass.

Those legs—the definition of his hamstrings, his quads, his calves...

The trainer in me wants to fall to my knees and worship every inch of finely tuned muscle.

The woman in me wants *him* to fall to his knees and worship every inch of me.

I swallow hard, divert my gaze—oh look, who knew the dumbbells were so interesting?

But when nothing happens for a long moment—no more words, no Knox walking back toward me, no phone call being made—I allow my eyes to drift back to him.

He's crouched now, furiously digging through his bag.

"What is it?" I ask, my voice high-pitched and squeaky.

He stills and his stare drifts over his shoulder, locking with mine, and the look in his eyes is so much like Evie's is when she gets into the cookies in the pantry that I have to bite back a smile.

This is serious.

We're trapped.

I can't be smiling at Knox Adler, especially when he says, "I think my phone is in my car."

That urge to smile fades.

Because even though I pat my back pocket...I know my phone is with my computer.

Both of which are sitting on the table out in the hallway.

Where I'd set them when I spotted the light on in here...and Knox working himself into oblivion.

"You don't have yours either?" he asks.

I shake my head miserably. "No," I whisper. "I don't. It's—" Cutting myself off before I give him a rundown of the exact placement of my work bag, purse, and phone, I turn away from the door and start searching the room for inspiration.

Maybe a landline.

Maybe an axe.

Maybe a flamethrower.

"It's what?"

Startled, I whip around, not realizing that Knox has moved so close. I flinch, snap out, "Back up!"

He stills, something sliding across his expression that

splashes over me like a bucket of cold water, but he backs up a pace.

And then another.

And *then* his face goes gentle, his voice soft. "Ivy," he begins.

No. *No.* This can't happen.

"My phone's outside," I blabber. "It's with my purse and gym bag on the table in the hall, so it's not accessible. But—" I spin in a circle, not spying that landline or axe or flamethrower.

But we do have medicine balls and barbells.

Inspiration striking, I move to the rack—

Only before I can snag one and start breaking the door down, Knox slips in front of me. I don't miss that his movements are slow and careful, as though he doesn't want to spook a cornered animal.

Doesn't want to spook *me*.

"Take a breath," he says quietly.

"Don't tell me what to do," I grit out.

That softness fades—thank God—and he all but wrenches the barbell out of my hands. "Jesus Christ, lioness. We're not going to bust down the door." A beat. "At least not until we've explored other options."

"There's no door handle," I mutter. "And we don't have a phone to call for help." I reach for the barbell again. "What other options can you possibly think we have?"

"No, I don't have my phone—"

"Exactly." I grasp the end of the metal bar, draw it toward me.

"But I *do*—" He tugs it away from me, easily, like he's taking candy from a baby. And it sends me spinning again, the fact that he's so strong.

I'm supposed to be the strong one.

I'm supposed to be strong enough to always keep myself safe.

I couldn't do it then—

My eyes close for a half-second.

I couldn't do it in the office with fucking *Hiller*—

I can't be strong enough to protect myself from Knox.

Even as that truth is tearing through me, blasting through the cracked foundation I've tried so hard to reinforce over the years, even as I'm reeling, I hear—

"But I *do* have a smart watch."

That has my arm dropping to my side, panic fading enough for me to rasp out. "You do?"

"Yes."

"Oh." It's a whisper, but he hears it anyway, his lips turning up.

"Yeah. *Oh.*" His eyes drift to mine and even if that soft understanding from before is tempered with amusement, I don't miss the careful way he asks, "Cool if I call maintenance then?"

I nod.

And then I step away, work on rebuilding my supports, my distance as I listen to him make the call.

When he hangs up after being assured that someone will be right over, the silence that falls is terrible.

Because I feel vulnerable.

Not strong.

Weak and pathetic and—

"I think I'm adopting a dog."

That snaps me out of my spiraling, and I spin toward him, brows shooting up. "*You?*"

He scowls. "Yes, me." A beat. "And I guess there's no *think.* I've adopted her."

"But...*you're* adopting a dog?"

The lines around his mouth deepen. "You don't have to sound so shocked, lioness. I've kept myself alive this long, and it's not like it's rocket science. Food. Walks. Toys. Good enough."

There's something about the edgy recitation that calls to the hidden parts of me.

Prickly and trying to put me off from seeing what's really making him feel off kilter.

Something inside...unlocks.

Because I think this is the first time that I've ever felt like I had anything in common with loose cannon, flies by the seat of his pants, never met a joke he doesn't love, nothing fazes him Knox Adler.

"I thought you didn't like commitment," I murmur. His womanizing ways are notorious with the team.

His broad shoulders lift and fall on a shrug. "I don't."

"But…a dog?"

"I couldn't just leave her there."

"Where's *there?*"

"The vet's office."

"Why not?" I ask. "That seems safe enough."

"Winter was alone on the side of the road, beaten and tossed into a snow bank with a broken fucking leg and cuts all over her body."

The anger in his words is intense, but also…not directed at me. So, instead of fear, I'm feeling…respect.

Admiration.

No. *No.* Such a slippery freaking slope.

"So, safe or not," he says, his tone still sharp. "I couldn't fucking leave her alone in a cold, sterile vet's office."

I have the feeling that the temperature isn't what he takes issue with.

But I—wisely, thank me very much—don't touch that part. "Someone left her in a snow bank?"

He nods tersely.

"And you found her?"

He nods again.

"And now you're keeping her?"

Another nod.

"You?" I ask again, but I do it mostly because this bit of news has settled somewhere inside me, somewhere I can't allow it to penetrate, and so I need to make sure he stays out of that vulnerable place.

Unfortunately, it doesn't work that way.

His head shoots up, his eyes connecting with mine, studying me for a long, long moment. "Yeah," he eventually says. "I decided I'm keeping her."

He's talking about the dog.

I know that.

But, also, some part of me thinks that he could maybe, possibly, be talking about me.

"Knox."

He prowls closer, not stopping until the toes of his shoes are brushing against mine. "Why did you flinch earlier?" he asks quietly.

"*Knox.*"

"Has someone hurt you?" Danger flickers through his deep blue eyes.

"I—"

"Don't answer that," he mutters, lightly cupping my jaw. "Or don't lie to me." His fingers flex, oh so gently. "I can already see it's true."

"That's not—"

His thumb brushes over my bottom lip. "Don't even try it, lioness."

"I—"

"I know you don't like me"—another brush and my pussy goes damp—"but I don't think you've really ever taken the chance to know me."

"I-I know you well enough." I lift my chin. "I know your type."

His body drifts closer. "Hmm. I don't think so, lioness."

My breath shudders out of me. "Knox…"

"I like it when you say my name like that."

"*Knox.*"

"And like that."

"We can't," I begin breathlessly. "*I* can't…"

"Because you don't like me."

God, no.

Because I like you too much.

Thank God, I keep those words in.

Thank God, I keep those words in *and* hear the sound of movement on the other side of the door.

But I kind of hate the way they change his face.

"I don't *not* like you," I say. "I just—"

"You just what?"

"Knox!" The voice echoes through the wood. "Are you guys clear of the door?"

He's gone still, every muscle taut, his eyes burning into mine.

"I can't," I whisper.

His fingers flex again, but then he breaks our connection, hand dropping to the side, his gaze tearing away from mine, his body pulling back. "We're clear."

There's some clinking and scratching (and then some cursing) but within five minutes the door is open.

"After you, lioness," he murmurs, nudging me toward the hallway. "I know you're late getting out of here."

I don't immediately move. "Knox?"

His brows flick up in question.

I don't know why I say it. There's no logical—or safe—reason to do so, but I can't get his vulnerable expression out of my mind. "I think you'll be a great dog dad."

His eyes go wide, but I slip out of the room before he can reply.

As I'm reaching for my bags, I hear my phone start blaring with a familiar ringtone.

"Dammit," I whisper, aware of Knox pausing beside me as I dig my cell out of my purse and answer the call.

"Ms. Pierce?"

Only a principal's voice can send that particular blast of cold tearing through me.

"What's happened to Evie?" I ask, the words rasped out, my heart in my throat.

"Well…"

She starts to explain but, unfortunately, that doesn't ease my nerves.

In fact, her reply is what sends me hurrying off to Evie's school.

And completely unaware of who's following me.

CHAPTER SEVEN

Knox

I KNOW I shouldn't be here.

I fucking know it.

But I still park my car behind Ivy's and get out to follow her into the elementary school.

Her face during that call, the fact that she doesn't realize that I'm trailing her, even now, the way her hands shake as she reaches for the handle and yanks open the door...

Yeah, no.

I'm not going anywhere.

"Ms. Pierce," the woman behind the desk says, and I don't miss the slight sneer in her voice. And I don't fucking like it either.

"Where's Evie?" Ivy says.

"In Ms. Hearst's office."

Ivy nods and starts down the hall, and I send a hard look in the direction of the receptionist before I trail Ivy around the corner and through a door.

My temper spikes almost the moment I follow her in.

Because Evie's turned at the sight of her mother entering and—

She has a scrape down one cheek and...

A fucking black eye.

"Mom," Evie says, her face crumpling.

Ivy has her in her arms in a second, holding her daughter tight as Evie cries. "Shh, honey," Ivy says. "I'm here now. Everything will be okay."

The principal, a frumpy middle-aged blond woman whose name has *got* to be Karen (otherwise I'll eat my right hockey glove) scowls. "Ms. Pierce we need to talk." Her gaze flicks to me and her scowl deepens. "Alone."

I lean back against the door frame, cross my arms.

But I don't move.

And Ivy doesn't release Evie. "Anything you have to say to me in private, you can say in front of Evie."

A long, tense pause. Then, "I'm suspending your daughter."

Ivy's mouth drops open.

Evie's eyes go wide. "Mom," she whispers. "What does suspending me mean?"

"It means that you're being punished for your behavior and you can't come to school for three days," Ms. Hearst says.

Evie?

Sweet little Evie had done something so egregious that she's being suspended for *three* days while somehow also ending up with a scrape and that black eye?

Not a fucking chance.

I straighten from the door frame, move closer to Ivy and Evie.

"Explain," Ivy says, her tone like steel, exactly like when she's telling us to get our sorry asses into gear and to fucking just do another goddamned rep already.

Ms. Hearst leans forward in her chair. "We have a zero tolerance policy for violence in this school."

There's a taut moment of quiet as Ivy clearly waits for the

same thing I am—a fucking explanation and not a goddamned sentence that brings about even more questions.

"And?" she eventually asks, when Ms. Hearst doesn't go on.

"And your daughter was violent." She picks up a stack of papers, straightens them by tapping one edge on the table. "I've made the decision that the suspension will only be for three days considering that this is her first offense—"

"And the other child?" Ivy's question is filled with ice.

"Excuse me?"

"Well," Ivy says and the frost dripping off her words drops the temperature in the room by a half-dozen degrees at least, "Evie didn't get these injuries on her own. So," she presses, tone even colder, "what is the punishment that the other child is receiving?"

"I—" Those papers are shuffled again and restacked. "Well, the other child's parents have already been here to pick up their student."

I wait.

Ivy waits.

"And what does that have to do with anything?" Ivy asks quietly.

"Their punishment isn't something I can discuss with you."

"James shoved me first, Mom," Evie says softly. "He wanted to go first on the monkey bars, and I kept letting him go, but then he called Rylie a bad name and shoved her down so hard that she scraped her knees and started crying. And when I told him that wasn't nice he shoved *me*."

"That doesn't—"

Ivy puts her hand up, cutting off the principal, giving Evie the time to go on.

"When I fell I hit my face on the bar, and I was bleeding and James started laughing. I said he was mean, and he hit me, Mom." She touches her eye and winces. "Right here. Really hard."

Ivy tsks quietly, runs her thumb gently over the bruise. "I'm so sorry, sweetheart. That was really not nice of him."

"None of that changes what your daughter did in response."

My brows shoot up.

And so does the rage in Ivy's frame, in her voice. "And that was?"

"She punched James," Ms. Hearst says.

"I did," Evie admits. "I know I shouldn't have, Mom. But I thought he was going to hit me again and—"

"You protected yourself," I say, seeing the principal preparing to chime in with more bullshit and interjecting before she can accomplish that.

Ivy's head whips around, eyes flaring wide in shock, but before she can—rightfully—kick me the fuck out of here, the idiot behind the desk decides to speak again.

"Evaline didn't need to protect herself," Ms. Hearst says. "There are staff on yard duties to mediate these kinds of disputes—"

"And where were they when James was hitting and shoving his classmates?" I ask.

That has the bullshit drying up.

"Exactly," I say. Then look to Ivy and Evie. "Let's go, girls."

The principal starts to stutter. "A-and where do you think you're going?"

"Home."

"Th-that's not acceptable. Paperwork must be filled out and—"

"Look, lady. I play for the Sierra," I say, no shame in pulling out the big guns. "Evie, Ivy, and I are going to speak with the team's legal department before we agree to any punishment." Her face pales but I press on. "And get some advice on sexist rule enforcement in schools and how best to go about pressing assault charges on a minor."

"He's six years old," she sputters.

"And so is Evie," Ivy says, murder in her eyes as she glares at me before she glances back to Ms. Hearst. "And if you're going to punish her then I expect that same punishment to be handed out to all involved parties."

"I'm certainly not going to be bullied into changing my decision by—"

"I think we'll also stop by the media team's office," I say slowly, tapping a finger against my chin. "I'm sure they will *love* to hear something about this. Stories like this go absolutely viral."

Ms. Heart's face pales further.

"What was the team's social media following last time you checked, Ivy honey?" I tilt my head to the side. "Four million?"

"Something like that," Ivy says tightly.

I flick my brows up at the principal.

And she caves. "Well, I suppose I could let this be considered a warning."

Ivy's shoulders relax, just a tiny bit.

"But if it happens again, we'll have to take further action."

"Yes," I agree, increasing the volume of my voice so the bitch at the front desk can hear me too. "Especially because what James did to Evie and her friend was absolutely unacceptable. If we hear that he's bothering her at any point during the school day then we'll be forced to consider actionable next steps—and those will not include tolerating unfair treatment." I look to the girls then tilt my head to the door. "Let's go."

I half expect Ivy to argue on principle—I've leaped over at least a dozen societal boundaries by coming here and jumping in —but she just nudges Evie back so they can both stand up then precede me into the hallway.

My eyes connect with Ms. Hearst's. "I trust that we will not have any further issues."

Her throat works, but I don't leave until she nods.

I catch up with Ivy and Evie as they're pushing out the front door of the school, pausing to catch the panel before it can slam in my face (and because pausing gives me another chance to glare at Karen Two behind the front desk).

Then I'm out into the cool winter sunshine, watching the breeze ruffling Ivy's and Evie's hair as I walk over to their car.

"Buckle in, honey," I hear her say before she shuts the back door and whips around to face me.

"You had *no* right to come here," she snaps, eyes flashing, words quiet but no less intense. "No fucking right to interject in our lives—"

I wave a hand. "Evie needs you more right now than you need to yell at me for overstepping."

Her mouth opens. Closes. Opens again. "Excuse me?" she asks, her tone deadly.

"I fully acknowledge that I have overstepped. But you can be pissed at me later." I nod at her car. "Go home, give her the comfort she needs."

She chokes, outrage roiling through her expression.

"Or better yet, get the kid some ice cream and remind her that you love her no matter what."

She opens her mouth.

Closes it again.

Then finds her voice.

"You are so fucking dead the next time I see you, Knox Adler."

CHAPTER EIGHT

Ivy

I'M SHAKING as I drive home, my rage at Knox tangling with my rage at that useless sack of a principal.

My baby is hurting and scared.

My baby was shoved down by a boy in her class.

My baby was *hurt* by that boy.

Why does this shit always happen?

"Mom?" she whispers halfway through our drive home.

I slide to a stop at a signal, flick my eyes up to meet hers in the reflection of the rearview mirror. "Yeah, love bug?"

"Are you mad at me?"

My lungs squeeze so hard that black edges into the sides of my vision.

How do I fix this?

How do I help her understand this isn't her fault?

How do I protect her?

...get the kid some ice cream and remind her that you love her no matter what.

The man is beyond presumptuous, and I'm equal parts furious and embarrassed that he followed me, that he heard me being absolutely fucking useless in that situation, so much so that he had to step in.

And…I'm grateful that he *did* step in.

Which makes me even *more* embarrassed.

And furious.

And…

I exhale, start with the biggest problem in front of me.

Making sure she knows she did nothing wrong.

"No, baby. I'm upset that James hurt you, upset that Ms. Hearst was being unfair, but nothing that happened was your fault, and I'm absolutely one-hundred percent *not* mad at you."

"O-okay," she whispers.

That out of the way, I check the road for cars, whip us around, and head in the other direction.

It doesn't take long to reach the ice cream parlor, and after I pull into the parking lot, I don't get out. Instead, I pat the passenger's seat and invite my little girl, my heart, my reason for living for so, so long to do her favorite thing—

Sit up front like a big girl.

"Really?" she asks, her eyes, even the one with the blooming bruise surrounding it, going wide.

I nod, and she quickly unbuckles from her booster then climbs over the center console, dropping down into the passenger's seat.

I spin so I can see her fully.

"Baby," I begin.

Her face falls. "You *are* mad."

I grasp her shoulders, turning her toward me. "I'm not mad," I tell her. "I'm so proud of you."

"What?"

"You tried to avoid a fight, baby," I remind her. "And when you couldn't, when he was hurting you and the people you care about, you stood up for yourself. How can I be anything *but* proud?"

Her eyes fill up with tears. "He started crying and ran to Mrs.

Donovan"—the yard duty—"and then I got sent to Ms. Hearst's office and she was *mad* at me. She wouldn't even let the nurse give me a bag of ice."

The rage that's been boiling in my belly threatens to boil over. "Is your eye hurting a lot, honey?"

She shrugs. "Not really."

My tough cookie.

I want to smile, to hug her tight, but I need her to know that I mean this first. "I love you, and you are strong and smart and incredibly brave. I don't know if I would have been able to do what you did."

"You don't?"

I shake my head. "No, baby. Sometimes I get really scared and I freeze, and then later I think about all the things I wish I'd said or did."

Like in that office.

Shove it down. Shove it *all* down.

Her eyes go wide. "I felt like that. When Mrs. Donovan got mad at me and then I had to wait in Ms. Hearst's office for you. I kept thinking I should have done stuff different."

"That doesn't feel very good, does it?" I wrinkle my nose, taking the opportunity to seize some levity.

She wrinkles hers in turn. "Nope."

"But you know what does?"

A shake of her head. "Nope," she says again.

I point through the windshield, see the moment she realizes where we're at.

"Really?"

"Root beer floats are the best medicine for a bad day."

Finally the last of the sadness in her fades away. "Can we get extra whipped cream?"

"Is it even a root beer float if we *don't* have extra whipped cream?"

A third "Nope." And she practically vibrates with excitement as we get out of the car and make our way inside, as we sit down and order the milkshake.

"Why was Knox there?"

Every cell in my body freezes, but I manage to squeeze out a semi normal sounding, "Hmm?"

"Why did Knox come with you to school?"

I know that I'll only get her to drop this if I give her some semblance of the truth. "He was with me when the office called. He saw I was worried, so he followed me over to make sure we were both okay."

Something like excitement crosses her eyes, making my stomach twist.

But before I can temper that emotion, our server comes by and sets the huge dessert between us.

Then we're too busy devouring the root beer float that's bigger than both of our heads to talk about James or Ms. Hearst or school or *men*.

Thank God for small miracles.

But that's the thing about small miracles.

They're small.

And short-lived.

As I find out when we get home.

Evie's settling into her nighttime routine, and I hop on my laptop, intending to email the principal and tell her that Evie won't be back in until a plan to keep her safe is put in place, when I see an email from Knox.

Irritation flares. Along with embarrassment. And a hint of tenderness that I pretend not to feel.

Especially when I open the message and see that he's pulled the contact information for the school board and superintendent and that he really *did* speak to the Sierra's legal team...

And a woman named Tera has drafted a nastygram of epic proportions that I can't possibly hope to top.

Fury.

I'm *furious* at him.

But as I scan that email, I'm also grateful.

That he crossed the boundaries, that he stood up for Evie to Ms. Hearst. That he's now given me these resources.

And I'm not so stubborn that I'll purposely withhold help from my daughter just to avoid a helping hand.

Even if that hand comes from someone as dangerous as Knox.

So, I wait until Evie's had her bath, until I've put some arnica cream to soothe the bruise around her eye and given her some pain medicine to help the headache that's creeping in (and I do all of this while also sneaking some pictures of the injuries James caused her, as Tera from the legal team advised in that note Knox forwarded). I wait until all of that is done and Evie's fallen asleep in my bed (because we both need that closeness tonight) to step beyond the fury, albeit just for a moment.

I copy and paste the pertinent parts from the legal team and send my email to Ms. Hearst, cc'ing every higher up from the superintendent on up to the school board, only pausing to take note of the superintendent's last name.

Because it's the same as one of my private client's.

And if there *is* a connection there…

Well, I'll use that too.

And then there's no putting it off.

I reply to Knox.

I *thank* Knox.

And I do it knowing I've exposed a huge chink in my armor to the person who, very likely, can hurt me deeper than anyone's ever done before.

CHAPTER NINE

Knox

"Ruff!"

It's not the loudest bark I've heard in my lifetime. It's not even the loudest bark I've heard this morning.

But it's demanding enough that I slip my phone into my pocket, that I stop thinking about the email from Ivy that I woke up to this morning.

It was short and simple without the barest hint of intimacy we had in the weight room.

But *she'd* emailed *me*.

And that...

Well, it feels like I've won something.

Fucking finally.

And it's...

Terrifying.

Because Ivy will never just be a quick fuck.

Because from the moment I saw her, I've wanted to claim her as my own.

"Grrr."

Kind of like someone else.

Lips quirking, I glance down at Winter. "Am I ignoring you, pup?"

She stares at me balefully before deigning to allow me to scratch her carefully on the top of her head. She's on the mend, recovering well from the surgery, though she'll be in the cast for weeks more yet. Still, the tech that's been working with her gave me a positive report when I came in—she's eating and drinking and today she actually stood up and walked for a few paces in the grassy area out back.

"She's doing better."

I'd felt Dr. Karlson approach, and I turn to smile up at her then shift over so she can sit next to me on the floor in front of Winter's kennel.

"All because of you guys," I say, running a gentle finger through the fringe between Winter's eyes.

The pup sighs, her eyes sliding closed, clearly exhausted by those few paces in the yard.

"We did our part, but she's a fighter."

I think of the tiny lump of fur I found half frozen and shivering.

"Yeah, she is."

"And also because she has something to live for."

"What's that?" I ask absently as Winter shifts a little closer, searching out more scratches. "All the treats she can stomach?"

"Yes." A beat. "But also…you."

My stomach tightens and I experience the urge to get up and walk out, the reminder that I can so fucking easily fuck this up and now an innocent creature will be in the crosshairs of my fucked-up-ness swelling up and threatening to take over.

"I didn't do anything."

Dr. Karlson opens her mouth, but before she can speak, someone calls her name. Sighing, she pushes to her feet then pauses and pats me on the shoulder. "Winter will be ready to go home by the end of the week."

I nod but force a smile even as dread builds up in my stomach. "I'll be ready for her."

Winter will have all the treats she can handle, nice beds, long walks (when she's able) and far too many toys.

I can give her that much.

Of course, it's giving her all the rest of it that I'm really worried about.

Because I think that part of me—the part that might be able to give more—was shattered decades ago.

I PUSH through the door to the rink and pause.

There's a little girl sitting in the hallway, her nose in a book, her legs swinging back and forth, back and forth.

"Hey, short stuff," I call.

Her head comes up, and the rage I feel at the sight of that black eye...

It takes everything in me to shove it down, to relax my hands that have clenched into fists at my sides, to not turn right the fuck around and go and find that asshole of a principal. I'd say find that asshole of a kid, but he's a fucking kid, and yeah, he needs to be punished because he's an asshole, but I can't reasonably be okay with punching out a child.

That bitch of a principal on the other hand...

Right, not okay with punching her out either.

But I'd definitely be okay to run interference while Ivy took the honors.

Evie smiles. "Hey, Knox."

"Whatcha doing?"

"Reading." A beat. "Whatch *you* doing?"

My lips twitch. "Getting ready to play some hockey."

"Mom said you had practice."

"Yup," I say.

"Then what?"

"Then we'll have a quick workout with your mom, and you can go home."

She shrugs. "I like it here." Her gaze swivels forward, legs swinging back and forth, back and forth again. "It's better than recess."

Poor kid.

Recess was definitely the best part of school—of course, I didn't have an asshole kid shoving me down and punching me.

"Because of James?"

Another shrug. "He's mean."

"It sounds like it." I lean back against the wall next to her. "Is there anyone else who's mean?"

"Mrs. Jamieson yells sometimes but she's mostly nice."

"Is that your teacher?"

"Yup."

"And your friends are nice to you too?"

She nods. "And Mrs. Phillips is *really* nice."

"Who's she?"

"Our music teacher. She sings songs with us, and she can play the piano really *really* well. And she can even play the trumpet."

"She sounds really talented."

Evie nods in earnest now. "She told me that when I get to fifth grade, I can learn to play an instrument too. I want to play the saxophone or maybe the drums."

"I'm sure your mom would love that," I say dryly, forgetting that Evie's smart as a whip and with high emotional intelligence.

She picks up on sarcasm and has a mind for details.

"It'll make her ears hurt."

I grin, but that grin fades when she asks, "Did you really talk to your lawyers?"

"Yeah."

"And they're gonna kick James out of school?"

I exhale quietly. "I don't think they'll get James kicked out, but I needed to do something."

"Why?"

"Because kids can be jerks sometimes, and if the adults around them don't hold them accountable for their mistakes then they don't learn."

Her lips press flat, but I don't get the sense that she's unhappy.

More that she's concentrating.

And her next words confirm that. "Like when I lied to my mom about putting my glass of milk in the sugar container."

My brows shoot up because...

Disgusting.

But also...why?

"I don't like milk," Evie goes on, "but instead of telling my mom that, I..." She screws up her face.

"Poured it in the sugar container?"

"Yup." Her nose wrinkles. "And boy did it smell bad."

I laugh. "I bet it did."

"And Mom made me clean it." She shudders. "It was awful."

"I bet."

A strand of hair slips out of her braid, and she shoves it out of her face in an aggrieved action that I've so often seen her mom make that for a second, I forget who I'm with.

She looks *so* much like her mom.

Only without the weight of the world on her shoulders.

I exhale. "Your braid giving you trouble?"

She shrugs. "Mom says my hair is slippery."

"Ella's coming by after practice, you want me to ask her if she can fix you up?"

"Really?" Evie's greenish brown eyes widen.

"Yup." I push off the wall. "Braids are one of her favorite things ever. I'll text her now."

"Thanks, Knox!"

I tug that wayward strand of hair. "Anytime, short stuff. Now"—I start down the hall—"I'd better get to practice."

Her gaze immediately drops to her book. "'Kay." Her voice doesn't reach me until I'm about to turn the corner. "Knox?"

"Why'd you really come to school yesterday?"

"I was worried about you and your mom."

Her eyes hold mine, and I have the impression that this is one of those moments when her emotional IQ is off the charts.

"'Kay," she says again.

Then her stare drops back to her book.

And I'm clearly dismissed.

Lips curving—and pretending I'm not in the least bit unnerved by that penetrating stare—I head to the locker room.

"Yo, Knox!" Storm calls the moment I clear the doorway. "You learn how to use door handles yet?"

Jesus, I'm never going to hear the end of this, am I?

CHAPTER TEN

Ivy

I LEAN AGAINST THE WALL, my hand clamped to my chest as I try to pretend that I wasn't eavesdropping...

And that I wasn't touched by the conversation Knox just had with my daughter.

And—

That I'm not feeling guilty.

Because I can't give her that.

Man Stuff.

Dad Stuff.

I can talk to her about her problems, commiserate about asshole kids, be pissed as fuck about what happened to her, be her Mama Bear and do my best to protect her from the world.

But I'm just me. And that's all it will ever be.

I inhale. Exhale.

It's all I'll ever allow it to be.

I push off the wall, bury my feelings—I'm good at that—and walk around the corner. Evie's still sitting where I left her a half hour ago, her nose in her book, her legs swinging back and forth. "Hey, buttercup, I'm ready for you now."

It takes her a moment to lift her head, her finger marking her place on the page. "Can I stay here?" she asks.

I consider that.

I want her safely in my office, away from any potential run-ins with—

I shake my head.

But also...this is the hallway that leads to the locker room, to the weight room.

She'll be closer to me.

To Kn—

To *me*.

I grind my teeth together, shove that down, and ruffle Evie's hair, further dislodging her braid. "Okay. But if you decide to head to my office, find me in the weight room and let me know, okay?"

"'Kay."

A kiss to the top of her head before I head off to get ready for the workout.

Some of the guys will be on the ice, and others will start in the gym. Most will hit both places at some point, swapping out with various groups, depending on who the coaches want to work with. My job is to supplement that, make certain the guys who need rest get it, ensure that the others who need pushing—unfortunately we have a fair amount of guys on the roster who need that—

Not Knox.

Ugh.

And not Lake or Riggs or Storm. Not Bear or Leo or Colt.

Just...

The rest of them.

And I know it comes from the top.

That slow rot.

It starts with a comment, builds with silence, with complacency, and pretty soon it eats away at everything good.

I'll leave before then.

Right now it's...tolerable.

So long as I keep telling myself that.

I resist the urge to fuss over Evie further and head down the hall to the weight room, making sure that all of the necessary equipment is present and accounted for. Then I check in with the team's head trainer, making sure that there aren't any injuries I need to take into account and make modifications for.

By the time all of that is done, the guys are streaming in.

I guide a group of them through some flexibility and mobility exercises, taking special care to activate the gluts and core—they'll need it, whether today on the ice or long-term throughout the season. Riggs starts in with a foam roller, targeting a tight muscle that's been causing him knee pain. Lake's on squats, lifting far more weight than I could ever dream of hefting. Leo's working on grip strength and Storm...well, Storm is doing his least favorite thing, but also the most important series of movements for him in this moment, at least in my opinion.

(And, well, my opinion *is* important because it's why I get paid the big bucks to order these guys around.)

All that being said, my young charge is getting friendly with his resistance band.

And scowling at me through every second.

I smother a smile, type up my notes, and I keep a watchful eye on everyone, tracking weights and sets and reps in my spreadsheet, stepping in to modify and correct movements as needed...just doing my job.

This is the part I love.

The part that brings me such joy.

Feeling like I'm making a difference, putting all my skills and knowledge and schooling to good use. Helping them feel better, perform better—

It's intoxicating.

It's why I'm here—

And maybe also because I can't afford to *not* be here, not yet.

"What crawled into your coffee today, Ivy?" Leo teases, sweat beading on his forehead as he hefts the dumbbells.

I smirk. "I think if you're talking that easily while you're lifting then you can go up in weight."

He groans.

My smirk widens.

But before I can snag the next weight up, I hear—

"Mom!"

I glance up in time to see my daughter running into the room, her hair in an intricate set of braids I know is courtesy of Knox sending a text to his talented hairdresser sister, Ella. She works her magic on the regular before Sierra games, and who am I kidding? Ella works her magic around everyone all the time.

Even more so now that she's dating Riggs.

And Evie is just lucky enough to be on the receiving end of that Ella Adler magic.

I wave, but before I can say anything, Lake smiles at her and wipes his forehead with a towel, saying, "I like the glitter."

My lips twitch. Because, swear to God, if someone had told me six months ago that the grumpy captain of the Sierra would be commenting on braids and noticing glitter then I…

Well, I never would have believed it.

But here he is, softened by Ella's best friend, Nova. She's just as amazing as Ella—a nature photographer who spent years traveling the world and seeing all sorts of amazing things, documenting them for magazines and online news sites.

And now Lake is complimenting glitter.

"Thanks!" Evie says, lifting her hand and bumping it against the big fist that Lake holds out before she winds her way through the room and stops beside me.

"All good, peanut?" I ask, tugging lightly at the end of her braid.

"Yup! Ella did my hair for me." She spins in a circle so I can properly admire Ella's handiwork.

I make a mental note to find a way to repay her for all the braid time she's put in over the last couple of months. "It looks great."

Evie leans in like she's imparting state secrets. "She let me have *extra* glitter."

"I can see that."

"And guess what?" she asks, positively vibrating with excitement, dislodging a sprinkling of glitter.

"What?" I reply dutifully even as I smother a shudder.

Glitter that I can't wait to clean off Evie's pillowcase. And rug. And jacket. And her booster seat. And—

Right.

I'll be cleaning it off of *everything*.

But my daughter's smiling and even though I'll be fighting another round with the herpes of the craft world, I won't deny her the happiness, won't complain and dampen the mood.

Not over glitter.

And not even when she opens her mouth and makes her next pronouncement—

One that's a hell of a lot harder to sweep up and out of my life.

"I invited Knox to dinner!"

CHAPTER ELEVEN

Knox

I WALK UP to the front door of the little condo, not sure what I expected, except to say it wasn't this—

Homemade garland is draped artistically on the front door.

Something twinges deep in my chest—memories that I've long pushed aside threatening to swell to the forefront of my mind.

My mom, Ella, and I cutting strips of paper, gluing them together into colorful strands of paper to match the seasons—green and red for Christmas, pink and white for Valentine's day, pink and yellow, blue and green for Easter, red, white, and blue for the Fourth of July, orange and black for Halloween, red and orange and brown for Thanksgiving.

I shouldn't be here.

There's a reason I don't fuck around with single moms, don't fuck around with anything permanent.

This entire experience has been a lesson in idiocy.

It doesn't matter that the rest of the area surrounding the front door is decorated too. I can't care less about the heart-shaped placard that's propped up in one corner of the porch. Nor the fact that it's surrounded by pink and white lights and a collection of baskets filled with red, sparkly garland.

Nor that the entire scene is festive.

Nor that I'd never expect anything like this to be in the vicinity of Ivy and all of her badassness.

Then again...Evie and her glitter and braids.

It doesn't matter that it's not Ivy's aesthetic.

She's a mom. Evie loves all that's bright and shiny and sparkling...

So, it's here on the front porch.

The decorations.

And her love for her daughter.

And *that's* the point it becomes too fucking much and I start to turn on my heel, to get the fuck out of there, to stop this insanity in its tracks before it's too late and—

"Knox!"

I still, dread snaking down my spine at Evie's little voice.

At her excitement.

At *me* being here.

What fucking right do *I* have to be here? Stomping over boundaries, interjecting myself where Ivy doesn't want me.

First at school.

Then in the hallway.

Now in her fucking house.

And yet, I can't make myself do anything but spin around and greet Evie like she deserves—with a big smile and enthusiasm. "Short stuff!" I exclaim. "I didn't think I had the right house."

"Why?" Her brows pull together.

I hitch my head at the decorations. "Not nearly enough glitter."

"That's what *I* said, but my mom said there was already more than enough sparkles for her to sweep up."

My lips twitch.

And then all thoughts of leaving and escaping slide out of my mind.

Namely because Evie's snagging my hand and dragging me forward into the house, calling, "Knox is here, Mom!"

I catch a glimpse of deep red hair and concerned brown eyes before Evie keeps towing me along. "I'm going to show Knox my room."

Me. In a kid's room.

Umm...

But I don't have a chance to get out of it because then we're barreling through a door and...

I'm assaulted by an explosion of pink.

My God. My eyes.

Did I know this many shades of pink existed? Logically, yes. Same as the amount of glitter on the curtains and the walls, the artwork and even the pillows sitting on the bed.

But experiencing it like it's an immersive art exhibit?

Yeah, not so much.

"Do you like it?"

I step inside, spinning in a circle, taking it all in. "I think it's the most Evie room I've ever seen in my life."

"My mom says it makes her head hurt."

"It does have a certain...brightness."

She smiles wide, flopping back onto her bed with her arms spread wide. "I love it!"

Grinning, I move over to the bulletin board—pink, of course, and covered in a crisscross pattern of gold, glittering ribbons. It's filled with photos of Ivy and Evie and my heart squeezes as I look through the collage.

Baby Evie in a tired looking Ivy's arms.

Evie in a tutu and tiara.

Evie and Ivy covered in flour and laughing, a sheet pan filled with misshapen cookies between them.

Evie with those glitter-covered braids and a Sierra jersey.

Evie in a karate uniform, holding a big ass trophy.

Evie at a concert for a big time pop singer even *I've* heard of —Jade Cantrell.

A life in pictures—a full, beautiful life that this little girl deserves. And yet, I have the sense that it's all for Evie.

What's it been like for Ivy?

Who's looking out for her?

Where are her special memories? The small moments just for her? The concerts or nights out or....well, not ballet classes complete with tutus and tiaras, but hitting a PR in the gym or going on a hike or hanging out on the beach.

Where's the evidence of what *Ivy* loves?

I wonder...

Well, damn, I know that—

There isn't any.

"We got first place."

I blink, not having realized that Evie's come close. "What's that, kiddo?"

She points to the picture of her that I've missed—Evie in some sort of dance outfit, clutching a ribbon. "We won our dance competition," she says. "We did the sailor dance."

I see now that the hat she's wearing in the photograph is distinctly nautical, same as the blue and white costume.

"What about that one?" I ask, pointing at another.

She scowls. "We didn't win that one."

Competitive spirit. I have to respect the hustle. "Did you have fun?"

She nods. "I *always* have fun at dance."

"That's good."

"Do you like my mom?"

I freeze, not knowing what to say—yes, I want to see her naked isn't exactly appropriate conversation for a six-year-old. Neither is yes, but I'm too fucking chicken shit to do anything about it. Luckily, I find I don't have to come up with anything more than, "Yes."

"Good." Evie spins around, flouncing over to her bed and

picking up a stuffed bunny. "This is Mr. Hoppity."

"Nice to meet you, Mr. Hoppity," I say, patting him gently on the head.

She giggles. Then skips over to her desk, picking up a coloring book and some markers. "Want to color?"

"Sure," I say, "but should we take it back out into the front room, so we can help your mom with dinner?"

"Okay!"

She tucks her book under her arm and heads for the hall.

Only, Ivy is there, her expression unreadable. "Dinner's ready," she says quietly.

"Aw, man," Evie whines. "Knox promised to color with me!"

"Well, Knox needs to eat, kiddo. Hockey players work hard."

Evie takes a long moment to consider that, and though she scowls, she also nods. "That's okay. We can color after dinner."

And then, she's running down the hall, markers rattling in their case as she goes.

Ivy sighs. "Don't worry, I won't torture you with coloring. Just shovel in some food, and I'll get you out of here."

That's what I want…

Right?

But my eyes drift to the bulletin board, to those pictures of Ivy and Evie—mostly of Evie—and though I follow Ivy down the hall to the kitchen, I don't look for the first opening to escape.

Instead, I eat the surprisingly delicious meal of rice and chicken and vegetables that have far more flavor than anything I cook on my own.

And then I color with Evie while Ivy takes a call from the school district's superintendent.

And *then* I'm not thinking about making a quick exit or even thinking about staying within the lines.

That shit's been blurred to hell and back.

I'm coloring well outside anything I've outlined.

And I have the feeling there's no going back.

Because the Pierce women…well, they're mine.

CHAPTER TWELVE

Ivy

I SIGH, my head pounding as I come out of my bedroom, knowing that I owe Knox doubly so now.

Or maybe it's more than that by now.

That scene at school.

The email with contacts and scary legal language.

That conversation with Evie in the hallway at the rink.

Being charming at dinner and keeping her busy by coloring with her while I took the call from the superintendent.

Okay, I owe him far more than I want to.

Far more than is smart.

But I'll deal with it. I'll pay up. I always do.

Just…after dishes and making our lunches for tomorrow and checking Evie's homework and drafting another email to Tera from the legal department for the Sierra, hoping they can help a mother out.

Or scare the school district enough so that this shit won't ever happen again.

The lights are on in Evie's room, so I stop by there first, intending to tell her to brush her teeth and get her jammies on.

But she's already asleep.

And…her clothes are out for the morning?

And her room is clean.

I frown.

I mean, that's our routine, but the fact that my daughter actually has done it without me prompting her is…

Unfathomable.

I shake my head, then flick off the light and mostly close the door.

Okay, so dishes and lunches and the never ending pile of laundry and hoping the fridge isn't leaking again. That seems tackleable.

Is that a word?

No, I suppose not.

But at least those are tasks I know I can get done before I pass out on the couch tonight.

I head down the hall and slip into the kitchen, halting when I find a tall, sexy hockey player up to his elbows in soap suds.

"Your dishwasher doesn't work?" he asks as I'm frozen, absorbing the blow of him there.

The yearning it creates in me.

What's that meme?

There's no surer way to get laid than doing dishes or laundry without being asked?

Because my pussy is seriously on board with that sentiment.

"Ivy?" he asks, his eyes coming to mine when I don't reply.

I snap out of it. "No," I say with a shrug. "My landlord keeps telling me he'll fix it, but it doesn't appear to be a priority for him." I pick up a towel. "Thankfully, Evie and I don't make too many dishes."

His eyes hold mine for a long moment, a muscle in his jaw flexing, but he doesn't do anything except continue washing the dishes, setting them carefully in the drying rack.

I snag a pan, start wiping it off. "You didn't have to do this, you know."

"I know." He finishes the last dish then turns the water on and begins wiping down the sink.

Seriously?

How is a woman supposed to resist that?

"How did the call go?"

I sigh, tug open the cabinet next to the stove and shove the pan onto the shelf. I should probably have an organizational system for these, something more than the Pot Jenga I'm constantly executing each time that I put stuff away.

But I also know that's not going to happen.

Far too many other things to keep track in my life aside from proper pot placement.

"That good, huh?"

"They're saying all the right things." I rub the throb in my temple. "But I have the feeling that they're just trying to placate me. They told me they're investigating Ms. Hearst's actions, but they haven't put that in writing in any of my emails. And I just..." I shake my head, pick up a plate and start drying.

"You just what?"

"I have that feeling." I sigh again. "You know that one when someone's going to try and fuck you over?"

He's still again. And then he slips the towel and plate from my fingers. "Does that happen to you a lot?"

My lungs hitch, but I manage to shake my head. "No more than it happens to anyone else, I suppose."

He sets the plate on the counter, picks up the next and begins drying. "Why don't I believe you?"

I inhale. Then shove the feeling of being caught in a lie to the side. I've been through the same shit as countless other women. I'm no different. Not special. "I didn't thank you for your help with Evie."

"You did."

I flick my brows up in question.

"In your email," he explains. "And with dinner tonight."

"I—"

His lips twitch. "I know you didn't make the invite, but you didn't murder me when Evie did." One broad shoulder lifts and drops. "That's good enough for me."

"Knox," I begin.

"And don't worry. I'm not going to be an idiot. Evie's great. You know that she's practically family when it comes to the guys, Ella, and I. Coming to dinner and hanging out with her isn't cramping my style. She's an awesome kid."

The way he says that—the sincerity in his words that I can *feel*—it hits me hard.

Nearly as hard as the sight of him standing at my sink, washing my dishes.

All of that being said. "Still," I begin. "You didn't have to—"

His fingers wrap around my wrist. "I know I didn't."

We're close. *Far* too close. And my body is far too aware of how close his is, of how much that nearness affects me—making heat bloom in my belly, desire between my thighs, need...

Deeper.

Somewhere much more vulnerable.

"But why?"

"A truce," he whispers, not backing up, not putting any bit of space between us.

"Wh-what?"

"I want a truce between us."

My eyebrows fly up. "Knox, I—"

"Don't overthink it, lioness," he murmurs, running his thumb lightly up and down my wrist. "Just..."

"Give in?" I ask archly.

His mouth is very close to mine, but his body is even closer. Which is why I feel his chest inflate on his next breath, why I can practically taste his next words on my lips. "Yes, lioness. Give in."

I lift my chin. "I don't give in."

He grins. "Oh, I know. So...truce?"

"Isn't that giving in?" I ask, exasperated.

"No," he teases. "Consider it…a strategic partnership."

"But you just said—"

"I know. Don't forget, if there's one thing us Adlers are good at, it's talking."

"Spinning bullshit, you mean," I mutter.

A grin. "That too." He rests his forehead against mine, just for a moment, sending my pulse skittering. Then he straightens, snagging the towel and tossing it at me. "Now, you finish drying and I'll put away."

"You don't have—"

"Uh-uh," he interjects. "Truce, remember?"

"Ugh," I grumble. "You're annoying."

"Another useful Adler skill."

I sniff.

But I dry.

And then I show him where the dishes go.

CHAPTER THIRTEEN

Knox

"No, no," Joey says, after blowing her whistle. "I want you to make the cut sooner"—she taps her stick on the ice—"higher if you can, and then push hard with those crossovers to gain speed."

I watch as the team's other fiery redhead (albeit this one has piercing emerald eyes) demonstrates. She's no less graceful than Ivy in the weight room, but there's something magical about the way Josephine Banks, or Coach Joey, moves.

Liquid lightning on twin blades.

Grace and strength demonstrated through simplicity of movement.

"Got it?" she asks us and we all nod. "Good." She lifts her whistle to her mouth, the next trill setting the drill into motion again.

Bear grumbles from next to me.

He's a big fucker, tall and strong on the ice, but definitely not the epitome of grace, and he isn't happy about the drill.

But when his turn comes, he executes what Coach Joey

wants, though it's definitely more through pure dint than any sense of grace.

Unlike Storm.

The young one has skating chops and impressive edge work.

I swear that I've never seen someone so accomplished on skates, and I do this shit for a living. It's like they're extensions of his feet. He never has to look down, hardly has to think. The kid's running out here while the rest of us are playing baby Bambi.

Ridiculous.

I'm just glad that he's on our side.

"Good, Stormy," Joey calls. "Now try it again with more speed."

He does and Bear grumbles next to me.

"You're just jealous," I say lightly.

"Damn right I am," he mutters.

Tweet!

"Adler!"

"Good luck, fuck face," Bear says, smacking the back of my legs with his stick.

I grin, start forward, and all but force my body through the unfamiliar motion. It feels strange, awkward, especially at first. But by the time I've made it my third rotation through, I'm starting to get the hang of it.

Of course, Storm is about three levels ahead of us, and I don't miss the starstruck way he's staring at Joey.

Or maybe *love* struck.

Smirking, I keep working until my legs and body cooperate, until it starts to feel natural.

Of course, by then practice is over and it's time to hit the weight room.

Ivy's here—why wouldn't she be?

The truce had held the other night as we talked about Evie's school—and the potential of changing it if this continues. It had held as she walked me out last night, pink on her cheeks, her hands still damp from the dishes.

Will it still hold this morning?

I brace against the impact of her, trying to play it cool.

But I want to wrap her ponytail around my hand, tug her head back and feast on her throat, get my mouth on her tits that are held tight and high in that sports bra and tank. I'll peel the material free, bend her over the weight rack and—

"Adler!"

I blink, shake myself, ignoring my dick and look over at her.

Her mouth tips up. "Get going."

I nod, head over to the board and give the list of exercises a once over. When I look up in surprise, I find her smirking over at me.

She lifts a brow in question. "There a problem?"

"Nope," I murmur, heading to the rack and setting up for my first set. But when she comes by to check on me before I start I can't resist saying, "Did you forget that you didn't want me doing this exercise?"

"I changed my mind."

"Really," I say dryly.

"Yeah," she says quietly, adjusting the clips, making sure they're secure. "Someone might have pointed out they can be beneficial, especially when paired with the rest of today's exercises."

"Someone who?"

"An annoying hockey player." Her eyes narrow, but they're filled with mischief and it's fucking adorable. "But one who knows almost as much as I do about strength training."

I open my mouth to reply, but I don't get the chance.

She just winks and moves off, leaving me with a misbehaving dick and the knowledge that I'd give just about anything to experience that mischief while we're both naked.

I heft the barbell onto my shoulders, get ready to roll, but before I start squatting, I catch Riggs staring a me.

He widens his eyes.

I just shrug and play dumb.

And then I get squatting.

Knowing that the truce is going to hold.

It *has* to hold.

———

"WHERE YA GOING?" I hear as I start to push out of the rink.

"My car," I tell Evie, pausing to smile at her.

She's holding a book, as usual, and her braids are courtesy of Ivy.

How can I tell?

Evie frustratedly shoves a loose strand of hair behind her ear. "You're going home?"

"Yeah."

"Oh." There's disappointment in her voice, and I feel like a jackass.

I should go before I find myself invited to dinner again, before I find myself in even deeper.

The truce is in place.

That should be enough.

But I know it's not.

I know it won't be.

Mine.

"What are you and your mom doing tonight?" I ask, stopping and leaning against the wall.

A shrug. "I don't know."

"No dance?"

She shakes her head. "That's on Tuesdays and Thursdays."

"Oh," I say. "And no karate?"

"That's Mondays and Wednesdays."

It's Friday. "Oh. Right."

She runs her fingers over the edge of the book, fanning the pages.

"Do you miss school?" I ask quietly.

A shrug. "Yeah, I guess. I miss my friends. And math."

"Math?"

She nods. "I like math."

"And coloring."

Another nod. "And coloring. And library time and art and PE and—" She breaks off, her face falling. "Music time with Mrs. Phillips. I really like when she plays the piano." A sigh. "But I missed it this week."

Dammit.

I'm an idiot for bringing up school in the first place.

"Hey," I say, needing her not to be sad. "I'm not actually going *straight* home."

Her face perks up. "You're not?"

"Nope."

"Then where are you going?"

'You know," I say, tapping my finger to my bottom lip. "It's a secret."

An exasperated sigh that reminds me of her mother. "Knox!"

"Well, I *could* tell you," I begin. I tug at the loose lock of hair, tuck it behind her ear. "But then I might have to—"

"Uh-*hem*."

We turn to see Ivy standing in the hall, her arms crossed.

"I might have to…ask your mother for permission first," I amend.

Ivy glares at me.

"For what?" Evie asks, her eyes lighting up and it's almost as much of an assault on my heart as seeing the mischief in Ivy's gaze earlier.

Two sets of deep brown eyes that hold too much pain and hurt and shadows.

Two sets of eyes I've changed.

A fist wraps around my heart, squeezes hard, and part of me wants to make an excuse and leave.

The rest…never wants to go.

"Yes, Knox," Ivy begins, her tone threaded with ice. "What did you need to ask my permission for?"

CHAPTER FOURTEEN

Ivy

"OH, MY GOD!" Evie squeals. "She's so fluffy!"

"Easy, baby," I tell her as she moves to the kennel.

But I should know my daughter better. She's smart and gentle and knows how to behave around animals (something that's mostly due to a rambunctious and mischievous pug named Steve that Lake's girlfriend, Nova, owns).

She slows down and drops to her knees. "Hi," she whispers.

Knox moves next to her, reaches for the latch on the kennel, and I'd have to be dead to not feel the little tail wag the pup gives him.

"This is Winter," Knox murmurs, opening the cage and reaching to lift the pup out.

I nearly gasp at how tiny she is, at all the shaved spots and healing cuts, at the cast on her leg.

Knox said she'd been hurt, been close to the edge, but…

This was bad.

Really bad.

She must have been so scared.

My heart squeezes again.

Knox had saved her—I'm certain of that much. Just like I'm certain the pup knows it as well. I can see it in the adoring way she stares at him, in the trust she gives him when he maneuvers her into Evie's lap.

"Will I hurt her?" Evie whispers, holding so still, her face an expression of concern.

"Not if you're careful," he tells her, taking her hand and gently placing it on Winter's head. "She likes to be scratched behind her ears. Like this, see?"

I hold my breath as I watch them pet Winter, Knox calmly explaining her injuries, and what he's learned about her so far.

And when Winter glances up at Evie, little tail wagging, tongue darting out to give Evie a kiss under her chin, honest to God, I feel my eyes well up.

"She'll be so happy to be going home with you guys."

I wrench my gaze away from the sight in front of me and see one of the veterinarians has come up next to me. "Oh, I'm not—" My throat tightens. "That's to say... *we're* not. Knox is just— My daughter...uh—"

The brunette gives off a no-nonsense vibe, but she's gorgeous, naturally pretty with the longest, thickest eyelashes I've ever seen on another human being. "Winter's a fighter," she says, saving me. Then she sticks out her hand. "Tammy Karlson."

"Ivy Pierce," I say, pulling myself together. "Knox and I work together. My daughter"—I nod at Evie—"loves animals. Knox was nice enough to let her meet Winter and help him get her settled at home."

"Winter's a lucky pup," Tammy says quietly. "In more ways than one." She tilts her head to the front of the clinic. "I'll just get the paperwork together so you guys can get out of here."

"Thanks, Doc."

I jerk slightly, not realizing he's come so close.

She puts her hand out for him to shake. "I'm just glad that we finally got here. Bring her back in immediately if there's anything that worries you, but otherwise, we'll see you in a month to get that cast off."

He nods.

"What's wrong with the kitty, Mom?"

I turn my gaze to Evie. She's carefully cradling Winter against her chest, but her eyes are on a kitten in next cage over.

And, dammit, but there my heart goes again.

"She's okay," Tammy says. "Just sad and a little small for her age. Her siblings all went to their forever homes, and she's still looking for hers."

Evie's eyes come to mine...

And I feel that sinking sensation in my stomach.

The same one I felt when I was trapped with Knox in the weight room, when Evie invited him to dinner, when we came here tonight.

I exhale.

I could fight it, dig my fingers into the slippery hillside and do my best to cling to the grass, to not slide way, *way* down.

Or I can look at my daughter with her black eye, with all she's been through...

And I can just...

Let go.

———

I GRUNT as I begin to slide the box off the shelf.

"I told you I would get that down for you."

I turn to see Knox standing in the door to my garage. "Where's Winter?"

"She, Snowball"—what my daughter named the fluffball of a white kitten—"and Evie are bonding." He walks toward me, reaching around me and snagging the box with ease.

I'm strong enough to lift it, but he has the height to make it easy.

A flutter between my thighs.

A softness in my belly.

Dumb. Dumb. *Dumb.*

He sets the box down and opens the lid, standing aside so I can pull out the empty litter box and food dispenser I had from my old cat, Olive.

He passed when Evie was a baby, and life has been too lifey to get another cat...

Until today.

Slip. Slip. *Slide.* Right down that grassy hillside.

"Anything else?" he asks.

"No," I say, and he snaps on the lid, hefting it back onto the shelf then snagging the litter box and food dispenser from me. "I can—"

But he's already moving inside, striding through the kitchen and setting the box down in the corner of the kitchen where I left the bag of litter I picked up on the way home and filling the container.

I do the same with the dispenser and bag of food, placing the former, once it's full, along with a bowl filled with water on a towel in the opposite corner.

We need toys and likely another litter box.

Treats and a cat tree or scratching post.

Vet appointments—

That, at least, halts my inner list-making. Vet appointments are covered for the first year—paid by the adoption fee.

I roll my shoulders. "Okay, what else?" I ask, more to myself.

"Food, litter. Maybe some treats and toys, but those can wait until the next time you go to the store," he replies, clearly ticking off a mental checklist, same as me. "The doors to the outside are closed so she won't get lost." His eyes come to mine. "And she has Evie and Winter." A beat. "And you."

It hits me then. The decision I made.

It's impulsive and beyond dumb and so totally not like me.

I groan quietly. "What the hell am I doing?" I whisper.

He exhales as he comes next to me, leaning back against the counter. "The same dumb thing *I* did?"

"You didn't just bring an animal home with no warning."

"No," he says. "But only because she was too sick to come home that first night."

My eyes widen as I turn to face him.

"I tried to lie to myself." He shrugs. "But it was never going to be anything but this."

I think about Snowball huddled in the back of that cage, alone and sad and tiny…and I know he's right.

This was never going to end any other way.

"Winter's really sweet," I whisper.

Fingers on my cheek, my jaw, running forward, his thumb brushing along my bottom lip. "So's Snowball. Her siblings were terrors, always trying to scratch the techs, but she always hung back and supervised the chaos."

I chuckle. "Why do I feel like that's going to happen here too?"

One big shoulder shrugs. "Probably because you're right?"

"You just wait until Winter has four working legs," I tell him. "Then you'll have to watch out."

His lips twitch. "It's funny because you're right."

The giggle slips out of me.

It feels strange, sounds even stranger to my ears. I've never been much of a giggler, and fuck if I've had all that much to laugh about over the last years…

That this innocuous discussion triggered it?

Slip. Slip. *Slide.*

"You're so fucking beautiful."

Every muscle in my body goes taut, every nerve becoming radically sensitized, desperate for his touch.

And he doesn't disappoint.

His thumb brushes over my lips again, and he shifts until he's facing me fully, until our bodies are so close that one deep breath would bring our fronts together.

"Knox," I whisper, "this is a bad idea."

"Because you hate me?"

I inhale, and, yup, I'm gifted with the sensation of my breasts dragging along the hard muscles of his chest. My bra and shirt are no protection, lightning bolts of need shooting from my nipples down between my thighs.

From one breath. One touch.

God, this man is dangerous.

"I don't hate you remember?" I whisper.

"Then why?" he murmurs, cupping my jaw fully, tilting my head up, leaning so close that I can feel his breath on my lips.

"Why what?" I ask on an exhale.

"Then why do you act like you do?"

CHAPTER FIFTEEN

Knox

HER EYES ARE soft and warm, her body relaxed against mine.

But her words are anything but gentle.

"Because I want you."

Because. I. *Want.* You.

The truth is there in the bald statement, in the guileless eyes.

And...

Mine.

Fuck it.

I lower my head, close that last inch between our mouths, and...

I kiss her.

It's a gentle touch, the barest whisper of contact, but swear to fuck, I feel something crack inside me—

Or maybe I feel it glue itself back together.

She sighs, lips parting, body melting, hands settling on my shoulders.

And then the kiss isn't a gentle touch, isn't the barest whisper. It's...every *fucking* thing.

I weave my fingers into the hair at her nape, tilting her head back further, deepening the kiss until I can sweep my tongue into her mouth, until I can taste her fully, until I can revel in her kissing me back just as deeply.

She moans, and I draw her closer, cupping the lush curve of her ass, leaning into her.

Nails biting into my skin, her leg lifting, wrapping around my waist. I pick her up, set her on the edge of the counter, dick twitching when our pelvises align and I'm reminded there are only a few layers of clothes separating us from the best fucking thing ever—

Literally.

The best *fucking* thing ever.

"More," she whispers when I break the kiss, allowing her to draw in breath, and I press into her, groaning softly as heat spreads through my body, as my dick hardens even further, as—

"Mom! Look!"

A proverbial bucket of cold water splashes over me as footsteps echo down the hall.

I lift Ivy from the counter, settle her on her feet, steadying her just as Evie careens into the kitchen. "Mom!" she says, rushing toward us. *"Look!"*

Ivy's lips are swollen, her cheeks flushed and marred with razor burn.

Damn, I need to shave.

What happened to thinking I need to go? To stopping this before I get too deep?

Yeah, my dick says differently.

Or maybe that's my heart talking—

"What is it, baby?" Ivy's voice is neutral, calm, as though she's completely unaffected by the kiss.

And, ouch, yeah *that* fucking stings.

At least until I get a glimpse of her eyes.

Then my dick twitches again, and I have to fight the urge to not pull her close again, to not taste that swollen mouth and feel that gorgeous body against me.

Her eyes are molten, filled with fire and need and—

"Knox!" Evie calls. "You come see too!"

Little fingers wrap around mine, dousing my arousal, and a moment later, Ivy and I are being dragged out of the kitchen and into the living room.

"Look!"

I'm still reeling from the sudden change in location when I see what Evie is trying to show us.

Fuck.

My heart can't take this shit.

Ivy's breath catches, and one look at her face tells me she's feeling this as deeply as I am.

Evie drops our hands and moves over to Winter and Snowball, gently sitting down beside them. Gently because…they're sleeping together, limbs intertwined. Snowball's head is on Winter's side, and her tail is wrapped over Winter's still healing leg.

"It's not fair that they're this cute," Ivy whispers.

Evie snuggles down next to them, tucking a blanket over herself and them and nope—

I *definitely* can't take this shit.

"This is your fault," she hisses.

I rock back on my heels. "What? How?"

She waves a hand at the trio, all cuddled up and adorable beneath the fluffy pink—of course—blanket. Evie's started a video and swear to fuck, it seems like all three of them are watching it. "*You* did that."

"No, I didn't."

"Yes," she grits out, "you did."

"Did not." Bewildered, I hitch my chin in their direction. "And anyway two-thirds of the trio belong to you."

She scoffs. "So what? You're still the one who started it."

"Um. *No*, I didn't."

"Right," she says archly, taking my arm and dragging me from the room, not stopping until we're in the kitchen. Only then does she drop my hand, but before I can ask her what's up, she pokes me in the chest. "Come with me and visit the most adorable dog ever?" Her brows lift and she shakes her head. "It's *totally* your fault."

I grin. "You're cute."

"And you, Knox Adler, are a menace."

"Who, me?"

"Come meet an adorable pupper with me!" She narrows her eyes at me before feigning surprise. "And oh, look! An equally adorable kitten you can bring home!"

I lift my hands in surrender. "Hey, I'm not the one with the cute kid who met the cute kitten."

"Just the one who introduced the cute kid to the cute dog *and* the cute kitten," she says dryly.

My lips twitch, but this is fun, bantering with her, being close to her. So I hold it together, at least for a few more minutes. "I think this is really Evie's fault. She's cute and exponentially so when paired with Winter and Snowball."

"You're blaming a child?" It's an arch question.

She has me there, but I don't admit it.

"And anyway," I prevaricate. "This whole thing is actually good news, you know."

Her brows lift and the mischief in her eyes is fucking beautiful. She makes a *hurry-up* gesture with her hand. "Elaborate."

I glance toward the hall, but there's no sight of Evie and company, so I step closer to ivy, run my thumb along that delectable mouth. "They get along," I murmur.

A flick of her gaze to the living room before those beautiful eyes come back to mine. "Um, yes?" she says, and I don't miss the heat blooming in her expression.

"And they're all cute as hell."

Humor and mischief and heat—

The trio in the other room aren't the only thing that's irresistible in this house.

Ivy is adorable too.

And strong and beautiful and…

I lean down, rest my forehead against hers.

"Yes," she says, exhaling softly. "They're cute and they get along, but I still don't understand why that's good news for me…and the money I'm about to drop on cat paraphernalia."

A sliver of guilt slides through me. She's a single mom and doesn't have an NHL player's salary. "I can cover—"

I still when her hand comes to my cheek, but I can't read her expression. "It's not the money," she murmurs. "The team pays me well, and I have my private clients." A sigh. "It's not even that bringing Snowball home was impulsive—though, of course it was. And it's not even that I'm likely to have a plethora of pink cat accessories throughout my house."

"Then what is it?"

She shakes her head. "Evie's happy, and it'll be nice to have a cat again."

"So, what's the downside?"

The wrinkles that adorn her nose are fucking adorable. "I have more things to thank you for."

That startles a laugh out of me. "Is this about the email?"

Her frown deepens. "What email?"

"The one proclaiming your undying gratitude for me."

A sniff. "I sent you a message thanking you for the resources and for talking to the legal team. That's all."

"Hmm." I tap my lip, mostly because I love the look of consternation that action sends across her face. "Kind of sounded like undying gratitude to me."

"Ugh." She shoves at my chest, slips to the side, and starts for the fridge. "Did anyone ever tell you that you're annoying?"

I chuckle again. "Yup. Pretty much everyone all the time."

That has her gaze flying over her shoulder, connecting with mine. She searches my eyes for a long moment, concern in her deep brown eyes.

"I'm joking."

Kind of.

Being annoying to my friends and sister is sort of my superpower.

"Hmm," she says again, tugging the fridge door open and pulling out ingredients.

"So you're thankful for me," I say as she sets a cutting board on the counter and pulls a knife from the block, passing it and an onion to me.

"Dice those," she orders.

I salute—with the onion and not the knife, because I want to keep my face intact. "On it."

She puts a pan on the stove then seasons and starts cooking off some chicken breasts. "What's the good news?"

I dump the onions in the pan, start in on the carrot she passes me. "Aside from you having to be eternally grateful?"

Her nose wrinkles again, but she doesn't take the bait. "Yes," she mutters. "Aside from that."

"You're so fucking beautiful you take my breath away."

There's a blip of silence as her mouth drops open.

And, fuck it, I have to take advantage of that.

Leaning in, I kiss her—hard and deep and...*short.*

Because I'm not going to be responsible for ruining dinner or scarring the child in the other room.

I break the kiss, heart pounding, dick twitching, the urge to pull her close and claim her so intense that I have to retreat, have to find steady ground.

So, I go for humor.

And I go for annoying.

And I say, "The good news is that you're stuck with me."

A beat.

"And *not* because of a door handle."

CHAPTER SIXTEEN

Ivy

"AND YOU'LL WATCH OVER SNOWBALL?" Evie asks.

I'm standing in the corner of her classroom, warring with myself about leaving her.

Fucking *hating* that I can't keep her glued to my side forever.

But she asked to come back.

And that little asshole, James, was transferred to a different class.

Ms. Hearst is still the principal and Bonnie, the receptionist at the front desk, who clearly can't stand the sight of me, continues to work the front desk.

But James isn't in Evie's class.

And the superintendent has assured me that James will have a behavioral aide with him during lunch and recess, making sure he doesn't go anywhere near Evie.

It's not completely perfect.

But it's enough.

"I'll take care of Snowball," I say.

"And Knox is still bringing Winter by tonight after dinner?"

I touch her cheek. "Yes," I confirm, knowing this is part

nerves and part...being my daughter. She needs to go over all of the details, needs to understand what's coming. "We'll keep her while Knox and the guys are on their road trip. Think she'll be excited about the toy we picked up for her?"

She relaxes, the last of her nerves dissipating like so much smoke. "Yes! And Ella said she'd make a matching bow for her collar." She holds up the end of her braid—which I've managed to keep together and refresh this morning after Saturday's home game had brought Ella and her braiding skills back into our lives —and shows me the bow.

It's pink.

And sparkly.

Because that's also my daughter.

"I bet Winter will love the bow."

Evie nods excitedly then wraps her arms around me and squeezes me hard. "I love you, Mom."

"I love—"

"Oh! There's Rylie!" she exclaims. "I need to show her my braid!"

She runs off before I can finish my sentence and I stand up, lean against the wall, and watch her for a couple of minutes.

"Stay as long as you need."

I glance over at Evie's teacher, Mrs. Jamieson.

"And know that I'll call you if there are any issues."

"Thanks," I murmur, and even though the words don't completely make my worry go away, they do make me feel a little better.

More so when she adds, "*You*. Not Ms. Hearst."

"Thanks," I say again.

She nods and slips off, gathering the students to the carpet, talking about the day of the week and the word of the day and then going into a lesson about something called digraphs.

I don't want to leave.

But I know that I need to.

So, when they start reading a book about an elephant and a

pig who have to learn how to share their ice cream cone, I take one more look at my daughter...

And then I head out of the classroom.

———

THE KNOCK at the door has me glancing up from my computer and frowning.

It's nearly lunchtime and though I'm supposed to be working, I'm worrying instead.

Yeah, my computer's on and my notebook is open and I'm pretending to be reviewing workout plans...but in actuality, I've been sitting here, staring at my computer from the moment I got home after leaving Evie's classroom.

Only Snowball has distracted me and that was for a few scratches before she glared at me balefully and went back into Evie's room, claiming her sunny spot on the rug.

Knock. Knock!

I blink and shake myself, pushing off the barstool and striding to the front door.

A glance through the windows has my breath catching, but I don't bother delaying.

I just reach for the handle and pull the door open.

Knox is leaning casually against the post on my porch, ankles crossed, brown bag dangling from his fingertips, Winter tucked under his arm.

"What are you doing here?"

He holds up the bag, uncrosses his ankles, then pushes off the pillar. Crouching slightly, he holds my gaze. Then tsks quietly and cups my cheek. "I knew you'd be like this."

Before I can react to that, he's wrapping his hand around mine.

"Come on," he says, drawing me back into the house, closing and locking the door behind us.

I reach for Winter when she wiggles in my direction. "What are you—?"

He settles her in my arms. "Evie has school for a few more hours," he says gently. "We're here to distract you."

An emotion that's far too much like gratitude spreads through my veins and I exhale, eyes stinging.

Dammit.

This man can't be here.

He can't know this.

He can't get this close—

"Woof!"

I jump at the sound then again when Winter's tongue darts out and she begins doling out kisses beneath my chin. "Knox," I begin.

"I've got Winter's stuff in the car," he says, setting the bag on the kitchen island. "Don't panic. Just think of this as me saving a trip."

"Because I'm worried about Evie."

His face softens. "Winter and I are worried about her first day back too," he says. "So much so that we almost forgot to eat lunch." He flicks his brows up. "Kind of think that might be catching. Though, why do I have the feeling you didn't eat breakfast either?"

My throat works, that warmth in my belly spreading.

Slip. Slip. *Slide.*

"Shit," I whisper.

"Ah"—he bumps his shoulder against mine—"we're in this together, lioness, remember?"

That's what I'm afraid of.

But I don't say that out loud.

Knox bends and scoops up Snowball, who's abandoned her sunny spot in favor of greeting him. He cuddles her until she gets impatient and because Winter's all but wriggling out of my grip to get down, I set her on the floor.

And when Knox returns Snowball to her feet, Winter makes

her way to her furry friend with remarkable speed, even given the cast. The two of them sniff each other and exchange kisses (or well, Winter is giving them out by the dozen). I watch them until the excitement dies down and Snowball moves to the bed Evie made up for her this morning, Winter close on her heels.

In less than a minute they're burrowed into the pile of cozy blankets.

Sunshine. Kisses. Cuddles.

And naps.

They're living it up.

"Winter's happy," Knox says, drawing my focus. "Snowball's warm. Now"—he moves in front of me and cups my cheeks—"are we eating lunch or are we getting naked?

CHAPTER SEVENTEEN

Knox

THE LOOK ON HER FACE.

God, it's hilarious.

But it's the pink that floods her cheeks that has my dick going hard.

"What?" she whispers. "We— I— Um— I—"

I grin and cup her cheek. "I'm kidding, lioness." I tilt my head toward the bag I left on the island. "I brought you Joe's."

She blinks once.

Then twice.

"Joe's?" she whispers. "I—"

"Turkey club with avocado and kettle chips, right?"

She blinks again. "I— How—?"

How do I know her favorite sandwich? Because I've been obsessed for months now.

"Let's eat, lioness," I say instead of telling her that and drop my hand to the side, moving to the island and tearing open the bag, reaching in to pull out our chips and sandwiches.

But before I can set them on the counter, she yanks the bag away from me.

"Um, hungry much?" I ask lightly.

She tears into the paper, stares at the bread, then peels it back.

Then she goes still.

So fucking still she could be a statue.

"Did I get it wrong?" I ask, mentally scrolling through my list of all things Ivy. "I can go back."

Slowly, she sets the bag down. Just as slowly, she turns toward me. And still, yup, *slowly* her head comes up, those gorgeous brown eyes drifting to mine. "Getting naked."

I frown, trying to understand what she just said. "What's that, baby?"

"Getting naked."

Okay, so I've heard her right. It's just that words don't make sense when paired with a turkey club. "Um…"

A step toward me. Another. "We're not eating lunch," she murmurs, dropping her hand onto my chest, just above my heart. Then she's moving slowly again, dragging her fingers down my pecs, my abs, my—

My breath hitches when she pauses at the waistband of my pants.

"*We're*," she says, slipping one finger inside to trace against my bare skin, "getting naked."

I shiver, fixated on that finger moving back and forth, back and forth.

So, it takes me a second to process what she's saying.

Okay, *more* than a second.

But, eventually, I get with the program. I snag her hand, tug it free. "Lioness, I—"

"Don't go all noble on me, Knox Adler. You asked and I'm willing." Her mouth tips up at the edges. "Now follow through on the naked part."

My dick twitches.

But I have to make sure.

"Ivy," I whisper. "You don't—"

Her hand slips from mine and descends, but this time it

doesn't stop at my waistband. She cups me, fingers wrapping around the length of my cock and squeezing.

I curse.

She steps closer, until her front is pressed fully against mine, her breasts soft against my chest, her thighs flush to mine, her hand trapped between us. "I want you," she murmurs. "I've wanted you for so long."

"I didn't come here for this, lioness. I just knew you'd be worried and—"

Her free hand comes to my jaw. "Knox?"

"Yeah?"

"I know you're good at talking." Her brown eyes dance. "But will you please do less of that and more of the whole getting naked part?"

It's the mischief in her stare.

It calls to the devil inside me, erodes any possible hope of control.

"You know," I say, reaching for the hem of her shirt, "I'm really good at multitasking."

"Oh?"

I draw the material up an inch, trail my fingers over the smooth skin of her abdomen. "I can talk *and* give you an orgasm at the same time."

"I think I'd prefer less talking and more pleasure."

Grinning, I tug at the material, dragging it up and over her head, leaving her in her simple cotton bra and a pair of leggings that coat her like a second skin. "Mmm," I say, lowering my head and flicking out my tongue, trailing it along the column of her throat, the hinge of her jaw, not stopping until I reach her ear. "Have I told you how beautiful you are?"

"Yeah, yeah," she mutters, though it's interspersed with her breath hitching when I suck on her earlobe, when I flick out my tongue again to tease the sensitive spot behind her ear. "Less talky, more orgasms."

I nip lightly, love that she trembles response in. "But sometimes talk is good." I press a kiss to her jaw, then to the corner of her mouth.

"Lies."

"Mmm." I drop my lips to hers and taste her, slow and deep, until both of us are breathing hard. "But what if I talk about how I want to peel off the rest of your clothes and kiss every inch of your naked body?"

She shivers.

"Or if I tell you that once you're naked, I'm going to get down on this floor and you're going to sit on my face?"

Another shiver, more violent this time. "Well, at least that would get you to stop talking."

I grin, slide my hand down her throat, trail my fingers over her bra. Then I'm pulling the material up, exposing breasts that are more beautiful than anything I could have dreamed up—and I've dreamed a whole fucking lot. "You'd think that," I say, cupping one of those gorgeous tits. "Wouldn't you?"

She gasps when I lightly pinch her nipple between thumb and forefinger. "Y-yes."

I lean down, until my mouth is just above her flesh, my breath a hot glaze on her skin. "And you don't think these words would feel good vibrating against your clit?"

"Knox—*oh!*"

I suckle her deep at the same time that my free hand slides down, down, *in*.

Hot flesh.

Wet lips.

I groan. She moans. And then we're both moving. She yanks at my shirt. I shove at her pants, her underwear. Her bra is tangled over her head. My sweats are down around my ankles.

It's a flurry of movement, not graceful in the least, but it's effective.

Because in that short amount of time, we're both naked, and the condom from my wallet is within arm's reach and—

"Woof!"

Our heads whip toward the animals, and I see two pairs of beady eyes on us.

"Yeah," I mutter. "This isn't going to work."

She jerks, but I don't give her time to reconsider, just snag the condom and scoop her up. The squeal she makes is fucking adorable. But I have other things on my mind as I carry her down the hall and toss her onto her bed, getting a flash of glistening pink folds and bouncing breasts.

I close the door and then I'm over her, spreading her legs and tossing one thigh over each shoulder.

"Should we see how good those words feel now?"

CHAPTER EIGHTEEN

Ivy

I'M REELING.

Trembling.

Needing.

And then his mouth is on me, and I'm not thinking about him talking or the accusatory look Snowball had given me in the kitchen.

I'm thinking about his rough hands gripping my thighs, keeping my legs spread and my pussy open for him to feast on. I'm thinking about the sleek darts of his tongue and the sensation of his beard brushing against me.

"Knox," I whisper.

"Fuck me," he growls. "But you're beautiful."

And *fuck me* if he wasn't right about those words feeling great against my pussy. They vibrate through my labia, arrow straight for my clit—

Or not.

It's his thumb and his tongue and—

"Oh, God," I groan, my head falling back against the pillows, my hips moving as I seek purchase, seek pressure, seek *him.*

And he gives it to me.

With his tongue and lips and teeth.

With his fingers.

With his—

Pleasure spirals through me as one thick finger slides home. And then another. And he's still talking, telling me how much he likes the taste of me, how much he wants me, how wet and tight I am.

All the while that pleasure is tightening through my middle, sensitizing my breasts, my skin, my pussy, my *clit*.

So, when he nips at the bundle of nerves, making me cry out, it's right there.

My orgasm.

"Come for me lioness."

Slip. Slip. *Slide.*

I give in, letting the pleasure come.

And God, does it come. Like a tsunami or an avalanche or an earthquake that razes buildings down to their foundations.

"Oh, fuck," I whisper. "Oh fuck. Oh fuck. Oh—" I break off with a moan, my vision going hazy, my limbs lax, my entire focus on how my orgasm feels as it barrels through me.

It may be a year later or it may be five minutes, but eventually I come back to my body.

And it's to find Knox still kneeling between my legs, his expression cat-ate-the-cream as he lazily trails his tongue through my pussy.

"Oh, God," I groan.

He hums then asks, voice a rasp, "Too much?"

Not nearly enough.

Even though I've just come, even though the aftershocks of pleasure are still ricocheting through my body, I want more.

I want all of him.

And I want all of him present, not the worry creeping into his eyes, not the hesitation entering his touch.

I reach down, snag his wrist, and drag him up, until our

naked bodies are pressed together, until I can feel the hard jut of his erection pressing against my thigh, so close to where I'm desperate for him.

"Ivy—"

There's worry in his eyes now.

I cup his face in my hands. "Not too much," I murmur, holding his stare.

"Then what?"

I allow my mouth to hitch up at one corner. "You'll never stop talking now."

The worry fades. Arrogance takes its place.

And the sexy smile he gives me has my insides pulsing all over again. "Damn right I won't."

"Shut up," I whisper, hitching my thigh around his waist. "And get inside me."

Heat flares in his eyes and need scorches the air between us, but he doesn't delay, reaching for the condom packet, rolling it down the hard length of his erection.

That he didn't hesitate to protect me, didn't give it a second thought from the moment we began this, unlocks another part of my heart, my soul.

Slip. Slip. *Slide.*

But then I'm not thinking about my heart, and I'm, sure as shit, not thinking about the past, about the bad men and worse times.

I'm not thinking about anything except for Knox.

He reaches for my other leg, lifts it, hitching it around his hip. "Hold on tight, baby," he orders.

I suck in a breath as he begins pushing into me.

I hiss out that same breath as he keeps going, as the stretch and burn of him pressing deep mingling with the aftershocks of pleasure.

"You're big," I whisper.

"You like it," he whispers back.

And then he gives me something I *really* like.

He pulls out and thrusts back in, hard and deep and a little rough.

"Oh," I murmur, grabbing on to his shoulders, digging my nails in, and holding on tight, just like he ordered.

"Yeah." Another stroke that has me moaning. A sexy smile that has my insides fluttering and pulsing around his cock. "*Oh.*"

He doesn't stop talking the entire time he fucks me, but it's not annoying. It's hot when he tells me how much he loves my pussy squeezing his dick, how he loves the way I taste and feel, and when he tells how I'm a good girl with a nice, tight cunt I know it's not going to take much to push me over the edge a second time.

Something he clearly sees if what he does next is any indication.

He snakes a hand between us.

Down. *Down.*

I gasp when he strokes my clit then again when he applies pressure, harder, rougher, more intently than before.

It's exactly what I need, that pressure, that roughness, and I cry out when he pounds into me faster, when his fingers work me, when he—

"Knox!"

"*Now*, lioness."

And my body behaves, my pussy convulsing around him, my orgasm blazing through me, my vision narrowing to just him and this moment and...

The pleasure exploding through me.

He keeps thrusting and it's a fucking beautiful sight, his muscles standing out in sharp relief, the sweat glistening on his brow, his strength and speed and utter focus.

On me. On my pleasure. On—

His own.

He groans as his thrusts go wild, his head dropping forward to rest on my collarbone.

And then I get to witness the most beautiful thing.

Not Knox coming apart—though that's fucking incredible—but it's what happens after that's somehow even better.

His gentle hands as he tucks me under the covers and holds me close while we laze there, dozing for a bit. His soft touch as we take a shower later and he soaps me from feet to shoulders. His careful strokes as he dries me afterward with a towel. His intense eyes watching me as we both get dressed.

The supplies he brings in from his car for Winter.

Him supervising the critters when I go and pick Evie up at school, then wishing her good luck at karate tonight—he knows that too?—when we stop by the condo for an after school snack.

Him telling me the landlord came by while I was gone to let me know a new dishwasher was going to be delivered and installed tomorrow—and the cagey way he denied having any part of it.

Kisses and gentle scratches for the critters. A sparkly stuffed toy in the shape of a pine tree that's the Sierra's mascot for Evie. And for me?

I get a hug and more words.

And they send me slipping further down that hillside.

———

THE NEXT NIGHT, Evie and I get home from dance, and I find myself turning on the TV, tuning to the broadcast of the Sierra game.

It's halfway through the first period and they're up on the Vipers by a goal, and though I'm tempted to sit and watch for a glimpse of Knox—

Slip. Slip. *Slide.*

—I go about with my evening chores.

We supervise Winter as she uses the bathroom, and then I talk Evie through dinner for the furry critters before making dinner for the non-furry ones.

Washing up goes a lot faster thanks to the sparkling new dishwasher.

Thanks to Knox.

And eventually, Evie and I both find our way to the living room, to the TV, to that Sierra game—me with my laptop as I tweak workout plans and look through my schedule for the next day, Evie with a worksheet on digraphs.

Knox gets a goal and is playing like he has rocket boosters strapped to his skates.

And I know that I'm watching the game more closely than normal, know that I'm giving far too much away.

But I don't know exactly *how* much until Evie sets down her pencil and glances over at me.

"Mom?"

"Yeah, honey?" I ask distractedly, holding my breath when Knox is knocked to the ice, not releasing it until he's back on his feet and chasing down the puck.

"Is Knox going to be my new dad?"

CHAPTER NINETEEN

Knox

"Hey, hot shot," I hear as we walk into the hotel.

The air conditioning feels good after walking through the warm evening air of Southern California. It's winter and it's eighty fucking degrees.

Lake smirks and claps me on the shoulder as the woman in a skimpy dress slinks close and plasters herself against my side.

"We won't count on you for drinks in my room, then," he mutters.

"No," I agree.

But not for the reason he thinks.

"Callie," I say, unhooking myself from her wandering hands. "How's the SoCal life?"

"Boring without you here." She steps close and reaches for me again then pouts when I sidestep her. "Knox," she whines.

"Sorry life is boring," I tell her, racking my brain for a way to get out of this conversation.

"Well"—she smiles and presses her tits to my side—"I know that *you'll* be very...entertaining." She drags a palm down my chest, and I feel...absolutely nothing.

Because it's not Ivy's hand touching me.

Not her body pressed to mine.

"Look, Callie," I begin, catching her hand and pulling it off me. "It's always good to see you."

Her bottom lip juts out further. "Why do I feel like there's a but coming?"

So fucking whiny.

Even when my dick was interested in her tits and ass and generous mouth, I still couldn't stand the whining.

"*But*," I say, stepping back again, "I'm tired."

"You didn't look very tired out on the ice tonight."

No. I'd felt like a fucking superhero, like I couldn't get tired no matter how hard I worked. The goal and two assists I put up on the scoresheet the easiest I can remember in a long fucking time.

And it's not because my body is rested, that I've got super strength—

If anything, my quads felt burned out from fucking Ivy yesterday, my back tight from the plane ride and sleeping in a bed that wasn't mine.

But once I got out there on the ice, I hadn't felt any of that.

I just...

Thought of Ivy watching.

Thought of *Evie* watching.

And I'd wanted to make them proud.

"Well, I'm tired now," I tell Callie. "So I think you might have more luck with the guys in the bar than in my room tonight."

She stills, pouty lip retracting, and the hairs on my nape rise when I feel her staring at me.

Callie is...

Well, great in bed but completely wrapped up in herself. She loves a hockey player because we "have stamina and great asses."

But I'm not the only hockey player she fucks.

Or *fucked*.

I know that. She knows that I know. And it works—worked —out perfectly for both of us.

So, her suddenly trading superficial for serious is...

Well, my stomach clenches and that high from the game?

Feels much more like a crash and burn.

I'm tiptoeing into dangerous territory. Or maybe that I've dived headfirst into it already.

"It's a woman," she says softly.

Yes, it's a woman—or rather, two of them.

"Goodnight, Callie."

Her hand settles on my arm, stopping me before I can walk away. "I'm happy you've found someone to love."

I freeze.

Because...*fuck.* I'm going to throw up. Yes, I've been enjoying the orgasms and the soft side of Ivy and how fucking cool Evie is. But *love?*

That's a treacherous step, and if I really think about it too closely...

I remember how much my dad fucked up with my sister and me.

And how much everyone always said I was like him.

How I promised myself I wouldn't ever step into his shoes with something as dangerous as love—because I don't want to hurt everyone I care about. There's a reason I swore off anything serious, a reason I keep almost everything in my life easy and free of attachments. I love my sister. I get along with the guys. I do my job and...

I keep it all smooth-sailing.

I keep it casual.

Until Winter.

Until Ivy.

Until Evie.

Because if I'm like him then they'll get hurt and—

Exhaling, I push that down. I don't want to think about it.

Don't want to consider how fucking obvious it must be if someone as self-absorbed as Callie sees the tangle of feelings—

Flying high to crashing and burning.

Cool. Cool.

Lips brush against my cheek, and startled, I jerk back.

"What the fu—"

A finger to my lips. A soft smile. Far too knowing eyes. "Breathe," Callie whispers. Then amusement creeps across her expression. "Don't worry," she says. "I won't tell anyone."

"I—"

A wink before she turns and starts to saunter off. "Oh, Knox?" she asks, pausing and glancing over her shoulder.

"Yeah?" I rasp, head spinning, heart pounding, lungs so tight I can barely draw in breath.

"Any advice on who's up for a good time?"

I shake myself and shove down the panic. It's fine. It'll all be fine. Ivy doesn't want anything serious—

She's mine.

I ignore that thought too and focus on something I *can* control. "Don't waste your time with Leo, Lake, or Riggs—"

"Or you, apparently," she says dryly.

I scowl.

She grins.

"And while the rest of the guys are single or looking"—yeah, that sounds as douchy as it is, but I'm not one to judge what some of the assholes on the team do in their relationships"— I think Storm is too far gone for your...charms."

Her nose wrinkles. "More's the pity. He's cute."

And currently moping over a beer in the bar, his gaze drifting —like it seems wont to do—toward Coach Joey, who's working on her laptop in a quiet corner, far too often.

"Look after yourself, yeah?" I mutter gruffly. "And stay away from Hiller"—our head coach—"he's an asshole."

She salutes, and I watch, my mouth curving, as she flounces off to the bar before I turn and head to the elevator.

Unfortunately, when I get there, I'm not alone.

Lake and Riggs are standing in front of the metal doors, and their eyes widen when they see me.

"No Callie?" Lake asks.

I grunt and shake my head, wondering if it'd be better to brave the bar...or take the seventeen flights of stairs up to my room to avoid these assholes.

"No talking," Riggs says.

"Thank you," I mutter, pulling my phone out of my pocket, pretending to be entranced with my inbox—

"No," Riggs says. "*You're* not talking."

"Exactly," Lake agrees.

"What the fuck are you getting at?"

"Something's up with you," Lake says.

"Nothing's up with me." I shove my phone away, stare at the box over the elevator and will the number displayed on the screen, indicating which floor it's on, to drop faster. "The game was fast. I'm tired."

"No Callie. No talking." Riggs shakes his head. "Something's definitely up."

"*Nothing's* up—"

"Ivy's up."

I jump and whip around to glare at Leo, who's appeared from fuck knows where.

"What's that?" Lake asks.

"Nothing," I snap.

Leo lifts and drops one big shoulder, like he's not casually outing me to my teammates. "Ever since he and Ivy got trapped in the weight room, Knox hasn't been able to keep his eyes off her."

"He's never been able to keep his eyes off her," Riggs mutters.

"Seriously," Lake agrees. "Man's been fucking obsessed since day one."

"I have not—"

They ignore me as Leo keeps talking. "Maybe so, but Ivy's started looking back," he says. "And then Jolie saw him"—a nod a me—"stopping by Ivy's place yesterday."

I choke.

Leo's mouth quirks. "Jolie does hair for Ivy's neighbor."

My temple starts throbbing.

"Apparently they were inside for"—he does air quotes—"*quite a while* and came out with huge smiles when it was time to get Evie for school."

That throb is full-on migraine now.

"Oh, and there's the fact that he laid a kiss on her that was"—more air quotes—"so smoking hot that panties were melted."

Riggs snorts.

Lake fucking cackles—and seriously, the man is supposed to be stoic and grumpy, not amused or cracking jokes like, "Finally figured out how door handles worked, did ya?"

I scowl.

Yeah, never living that down.

But, thank fuck, the elevator doors finally open with a ding. "None of you are funny," I grind out as I step onto the cart.

"Maybe not," Riggs says. "But we're all in the same boat, man. Just give in."

I *have* given in.

It's why I'm here now, listening to this shit.

Why I'm barely beating back the panic as I try to pretend what's happening in my head and heart isn't actually happening.

Mine.

Dangerous.

I'm going to hurt her. I'm going to fuck up.

I have to end this now…

I fucking *can't* do that.

"Seriously," Lake adds as he gets on next to me, bumping his shoulder against mine and jarring me out of my mental spiraling. "The best thing that's ever happened to me is finding Nova stranded on the side of the road."

"Same." Leo crams his way in. "Jolie stumbling into my path was the best day of my life."

Riggs shrugs and climbs on. "Don't be a dumbass like I was." He cuts a look in my direction. "Unless you need me to repeat advice that you once gave me."

That almost makes me snort.

Because I'd pushed him to date my sister.

The difference is that he's not a fuck-up.

He doesn't have DNA that means he's destined to hurt the people he loves.

"No," I growl. "I don't need advice."

"Good." Lake claps me on the shoulder. "So we can get straight down to threatening."

I whip around and glare at him. "What the fuck?" I snap. "Ivy hasn't done anything to you."

"I know," he says and before I can punch the fucker, his forearm is in my throat and he's pinning me to the elevator's wall, his eyes cold and fierce—the intense captain of our team in full force. "Ivy is good people," he grits out as the doors close behind us. "And Evie is a great fucking kid. Don't go there unless you can take shit seriously."

Panic twists my insides, but I don't back down.

"Ivy's not just some quick fuck."

She's more—and that's why I'm having an existential fucking crisis.

"No," he says, "she's just a hot piece of ass you'll fuck around with until you get tired of her. Then you'll move on and leave her hurt and—"

That snaps something inside me.

My control. My hold on my panic because that's my deepest fear.

My *temper.*

I rage forward, breaking his hold and reversing our positions.

He grunts when I slam him into the wall, shaking the cart, the floors flying by us.

"Don't talk about her like that," I growl.

Instead of shoving me back—or punching me like he's done to plenty of assholes on the ice—Lake just smiles and glances over at Leo and Riggs, who are staying conspicuously out of this. "He's got it bad."

Christ.

I do have it bad.

And all these fuckers are witnesses to it.

I drop my arm and glare at them. "You're all assholes."

The doors open with a ding, and my teammates clamber out onto the floor, dragging me alongside them.

"Maybe so," Riggs says as we walk down the hall and start peeling off at our respective rooms, first Lake, then Leo. "But you're still going to keep her."

Mine.

He swipes his card, pushes into his room, leaving me alone to walk a couple of doors down to my suite, those words bouncing around my mind.

And knowing that he's absolutely fucking right.

CHAPTER TWENTY

Ivy

I'M LYING IN BED, a glass of wine on the side table, and trying to figure out what I'm feeling.

And why most of it is disappointment.

Is Knox going to be my new dad?

I wanted to say yes. Or even maybe. Or there's a ten percent chance of saying perhaps in the following counties. Or—

Christ, I can't do this.

I grab my wine, climb out of bed and go into the living room.

Evie's in bed, and she didn't fight me, thankfully, but I need to be sleeping as well. I have to drop her off in the morning and then have a call with the superintendent himself to follow up about her first days back. A call I'm not dreading because I had a session with my long-time client this morning—the one with the same last name as the superintendent.

Turns out, it's not a coincidence.

She happens to know the man well because she's married to his brother.

But it's more than that.

Her sister married into the family too—and is hitched to the superintendent himself.

Small fucking world.

Especially since her sister happened to join in on today's session. So, when I told Darlene and Diana—the sister—about what happened and the red tape and lack of responsibility taken by Ms. Hearst, they flipped out, pulled some strings, and—

No more emails vetted by the superintendent's assistant.

No more dancing around and placating speech about having it covered and to just trust the district.

I now have a one-on-one call to discuss my concerns.

And I got to listen to the ladies read him the riot act at the end of our session.

Turns out, yelling is great cardio.

And now I don't just have the Sierra's legal team at my back.

I have Darlene and Diana *and*...the superintendent, Brian, on my side.

Am I pulling strings? Taking advantage of my connections?

Abso-fucking-lutely.

And I don't feel guilty in the least.

I would walk to the end of the earth and back if it meant protecting my daughter.

So no guilt whatsoever...

Until I remember that I have Knox too, that he's been kind and gone the extra mile and is sexy and sweet and thoughtful and—

Is Knox going to be my new dad?

I can't allow that thought of my daughter's to grow.

And I know what I have to do—no matter how much I hate it.

Temple throbbing, I sigh, take a long glug of wine, then do what I do every time the past wants to reach out and yank me back under.

I exercise.

Not to an unhealthy amount—not anymore, anyway.

I've definitely had moments like that, times where working myself into exhaustion was the only way to sleep without nightmares coming.

Now I know better.

The nightmares eventually come back, no matter how hard I work out or how heavy the weights or how far I run.

So...I learned.

When I killed myself in the weight room, I ended up hurting both inside *and* out.

There's a balance.

But there are still positives to a challenging workout, especially when my brain is slightly fuzzy from the glass of wine.

It quiets Evie's question that continues to ricochet through my mind.

Quiets the feelings.

Quiets the disappointment I feel because I already know the answer.

Because while I got away with distraction—Knox scoring and us celebrating with ice cream—I know I have to tell Evie no.

No, Knox isn't going to be her new dad. No, I'm never going to be open to another relationship. No, I can't give you what you deserve. No, I can't have what I—

What I want either.

My head throbs again and I exhale, moving over to the mat I've rolled out on the rug.

Then I run through the set of stretches and body weight exercises, easing my body into the familiar routine that keeps me flexible and strong.

It's muscle memory at this point, my own mix of what makes me feel good.

And it's challenging, taking all of my focus to hold the positions, to keep my balance, to stay in this place where I'm taking care of my muscles and nerves, my tissue and joints.

By the end, I'm covered with sweat, my limbs are shaking, and...my glass of wine is empty.

This is what I'm always talking about with my clients about hydration, right?

Smiling, I release my plank and flop back onto the mat, my chest heaving, my body covered in sweat...

And suddenly I'm right back to thinking about all the things I can't have—

Knox in my bed on the regular, using that big dick of his to bring me pleasure. Knox's gentle hands soaping me up in the shower. Knox and Evie coloring together while I cook dinner. Knox calling my landlord and getting him to fix my dishwasher—

"Enough," I groan, rubbing my hands over my face.

I take my wine glass to the sink, roll up the mat and stow it away, and...

Then I shower.

By myself.

But the memory of Knox's gentle touch skating over my skin remains.

And sleep takes a long, long time to come.

———

"BYE, MOM!" Evie says, running into the classroom without a second glance back.

Resilient.

I hate it and I love it—love *her*—so much.

What I don't love is turning around and seeing Ms. Hearst standing in the hall behind me.

"How's she doing?"

"Fine," I say because I'm not going to make unnecessary trouble. "Thanks for asking," I say and start to push by her. "I have to get to work now."

"With the Sierra?" she asks dryly.

"I do work for them," I reply, just as dryly.

"Right." She follows me as I start down the hall. "And aren't they in Southern California right now?"

I exhale, trying to keep my cool because I don't like the smugness in her beady, snake-like eyes. "They are. But I don't travel with the team, and when I'm here and they're not, I work with my private clients."

She sniffs.

Maybe I should let it go.

But I can't resist pausing at the gate that leads out to the parking lot and saying, "The guys on the team are great, but I really enjoy working with my other clients."

She frowns but takes the bait. "Why?"

"Oh," I say lightly, "because they're just normal people, not multi-million dollar athletes." I smile. "I get to know stay-at-home moms, retired businesswomen, ski instructors, nurses, teachers, and even"—I tap a finger to my lips as though thinking, but fuck it, if I'm going to drop this bomb, I'm going to do it in style—"family members of the superintendent."

Ms. Hearst's mouth drops open, horror creeping into her expression.

And, know what?

I haven't had too many wins in my life.

It's been a grind, a struggle, sometimes a fucking battle. This conversation?

For once, it's an easy victory.

So, I'm going to take it.

"In fact, I'm speaking to Brian this morning. I'll let him know how…" I lift my brows, allowing the silence to linger, and I'm not going to lie, the worry in Ms. Hearst's eyes, the way she goes completely pale—

Well, it doesn't make up for what happened to Evie, doesn't make up for what she was going to do to my daughter…

But it goes a long fucking way to making it better.

"I'll let him know how *helpful* you've been," I finish a long moment later.

And with that, I push through the gate and walk out into the parking lot, waving at her through my windshield when I see her still standing there as I drive off.

Of course, as is typical in my life, my feeling of victory doesn't last long.

Because reality returns as I hear Evie's voice in my head asking,

Is Knox going to be my new dad?

Stomach twisting, I navigate out onto the road and head for my first client, the cold truth washing over me.

I flick my eyes to the heaven, sigh quietly.

"Yeah," I mutter. "Thanks for the reminder to not get too cocky."

CHAPTER TWENTY-ONE

Knox

"You've been holding out on me."

I step off the bus and see my sister standing there, arms crossed, foot tapping, her expression full of sass.

Christ, I don't want to deal with this right now.

"Your man is right behind me," I say, going for distraction.

Which she doesn't buy in the least.

"Hmm," she says dryly. "No pithy comment about your matchmaking skills." Her arms wrap around me when I get close, words for my ears only. "Now I *really* know that Riggs wasn't lying about you holding out on me."

I roll my eyes. "Yeah, like Riggs has that many words."

A chuckle before she presses her lips to my cheek. "Funny." A beat. "Like always." Then she pulls back, hands on the outsides of my shoulders, eyes fixed on mine.

Eyes *searching* mine.

Fuck no.

I've had enough soul-searching of my own accord, enough friendly interference, enough fucking teasing and then encouragement from my teammates. Hell, I'm being so obvious that I even got it from *Callie*.

And frankly, if I stop and think about it, if I accept the feeling that's growing with each waking moment I'm getting back on the bus and riding the fuck out of here.

L.A.

Tahiti.

Antarctica.

Anywhere that's far away from here.

Only…I don't want to leave Ivy.

Or Evie.

Or—

Mine.

Terror grips my insides as I pull out of my sister's hold, my voice sounding strained, even to my own ears when I say, "I need to go get Winter."

"Yeah, about that—"

I freeze, know in my haste that I've made a critical error.

I haven't really talked to Ella about Winter.

Because I've been too fucking obsessed with Ivy.

With falling in *love* with Ivy.

A cold sweat breaks out on my nape.

"—when am I going to get to meet the new lady in my brother's life?"

"I—"

"And when am I going to *hear* about my brother adopting a dog?" she asks slowly, crossing her arms again, tapping that foot for good measure. "Furthermore, when am I—"

"Go easy, *cherié*." Riggs shoves me back a step, wraps an arm around her waist, and lays a kiss on her that should be illegal.

In public parking lots.

In front of brothers.

"Ugh," I mutter averting my gaze. "Get a fucking room already."

"We've got one of those," Riggs says tone tinted with amusement. "An entire house worth of them."

"Ew."

Ella just grins and shrugs at me. "He's not wrong."

If I hadn't set them up, if I didn't know exactly how much Riggs loves her, if I haven't been a witness to how well he treats her and how happy my sister is...

Well, murder would definitely be on the table.

As it is, it's already hard enough to remember all of that with his tongue down my baby sister's throat, let alone them talking about having an entire house of Fuck Rooms.

"What's up with the dog?" Riggs asks.

I exhale. "Nothing really. I found her on the side of the road. She was freezing cold and hurt, and the vet didn't think she would make it. But she did." I feel my mouth curving, know my voice is filled with pride. Dumb probably, to be proud of a dog, but I can't help it. Winter's a fighter.

"So you adopted her?"

"More like she adopted me."

Ella smiles. "Sounds about right."

"And Ivy?"

My heart pulses. "What about Ivy?"

Riggs snorts.

Her lips twitch, but my sister isn't as big of a pain in the ass as I am—or maybe she knows all the shit that I'm feeling, so gives me a pass, just this once.

She leans in. "You're not Dad," she whispers. "Never have been. Never will be."

"Ella—"

"And we're not our past. *You* showed me that."

"It's a fuck-ton easier to believe that when you're not the one in the line of fire."

Her mouth hitches up. "Believe me, I know."

"You're annoying," I grumble.

"Also something I know." She bumps her shoulder against

mine before Riggs snakes an arm around her waist and draws her back against his chest.

"Never, *chérie*."

My sister's face softens and she pats his jaw. "One second, honey. Okay?"

He nods, but his gaze comes to mine and I don't miss the warning. "She's worked too much while we were gone," he tells me. "And this morning. Don't keep her too long."

Damn, he's good.

Something I know.

It's why I pushed them to get together.

Christ, I want what they have.

But I'm a fucking coward.

"Knox," Ella murmurs.

I absently rub a hand over my chest, trying to ease the ache there. "Yeah?"

Her hand drops to my forearm and she squeezes. "Be brave."

My heart thuds hard against my rib cage, but I force my tone to be light. "Hey, who's the one who always killed the spiders?" I tease. "And checked under the bed for monsters?"

"And forced me to see past my fear of what could go wrong if I opened my heart to love so that I could realize how incredible all the right parts feel?"

Another thud of my heart, this time hard enough that it's nearly impossible to get the next words out in a normal voice. "You deserve it, Ells."

Her smile is bright and beautiful and bold—just like her. "I know." Another squeeze of my arm. "And soon enough you'll realize that you deserve it too."

"Ells," I mutter. "I—"

Squeeze. "Be." Another. "Brave."

"I—"

"Or," she says, "if you need me to pull out Mean Ella then I'll phrase it differently—shit or get off the pot, honey."

I jerk.

"Because if anyone could understand what we went through, it's Ivy."

What the fuck?

"And," she goes on, "if anyone deserves someone to show her—and Evie—how beautiful love can be"—she rises on tiptoe, presses a kiss to my cheek—"it's Ivy."

With that bomb, she drops back down onto her heels and turns away, heading for Riggs, who's waiting with Nova and Lake. They're probably talking shit or gossiping, and yeah, I'm grumpy about it, but I can't summon any real anger.

Mostly because I know that if the tables were turned, I'd be doing the same.

Hell, I'd be the *head* gossip.

It just sucks when *I'm* the one who's being a fucking pussy.

It sucks that I'm scared.

It sucks that—

Fucking enough.

My sister is right.

I need to stop being a pussy and step the fuck up.

"Actually, Ells," I call. "I do have a question for you."

She lifts her brows, starts walking back toward me. "What's that?"

"How hard is it to learn how to braid?"

Her steps falter.

But then slowly, *oh so slowly*, she smiles.

CHAPTER TWENTY-TWO

Ivy

THE KNOCK on the door today isn't unexpected.

In fact, it's planned.

Winter's sleepover is done.

Knox is here to pick her up.

Is Knox going to be my new dad?

"Ugh," I mutter, rubbing the ache in my temples. It's become constant, even though the call this morning went well. "Just *enough.*" This isn't complicated. Knox and I are...*sex.* Friendly acquaintances doing each other a favor at best, friends with benefits at worst.

Nothing more.

So, why did excitement ripple through me at that knock?

Why did I have to clutch the counter so I didn't hurry to answer it, to pull the door open and leap into his arms?

Why, even now, am I fighting the urge to just give in and see where this all goes?

Slip. Slip. *Slide.*

"I know better," I whisper, pushing up off the stool and bracing myself for the presence of him.

Just give him the dog and send him on his way.

Then Evie and I will get back to our lives.

And she'll forget about him, just like she forgot about that dad from karate...Tom, I think.

Exhaling, I move into the hall then reach for the door handle just as the knock starts again. I pull it open and—*fuck*—but bracing for him didn't do a damned thing.

My knees wobble and my pussy clenches and—

"Hey, lioness."

Oh, sweet baby Jesus.

He bends down, as though to kiss me and I jump back, hating that his brows pull together and a mix of confusion and hurt enters those piercing blue eyes of his.

"Snowball's decided she wants to be an escape artist," I say lamely, taking another step back.

Not a lie, but I still feel guilty.

"Ah." His lips twitch as he steps inside, quickly closes the door.

"Thanks," I murmur, turning for the kitchen. "I'm sure you're tired from the travel." I nod at the bag on the table I keep in the hall. "I packed up Winter's stuff for you. We just need to interrupt the fluffballs' mid-morning nap, which, of course, came after their morning nap." I flick my gaze over my shoulder, see that he's stopped and is staring at the packed bag like it contains a bomb...

"They're in Evie's room," I add quietly, trying to ignore the sick feeling in my stomach.

He looks up. "Right."

I start down the hall again, but I only make it a single step before he's in front of me, determination woven into his expression.

Shit. *Shit.*

"Lioness," he murmurs. "Is this because I didn't call while I was gone?" He touches my cheek. "I'm sorry. I know I should have checked in."

A bolt of guilt shoots through me, but I shake my head fiercely. "No," I say. "I was busy. I-I—" My throat is tight, so I clear it. "Evie has school and karate and dance, and I was busy with my clients and then I found out—" I fill him in on the connection to the superintendent and my call this morning.

"That's great news, baby."

I nod jerkily. "So, yeah, it was a busy couple of days. I'm not mad that you didn't call. You replied to the pictures of Winter I texted, and Evie and I watched the game so we knew you were doing well."

"You watched the game?"

That sick feeling in my stomach grows.

Because he looks…happy and proud and—

Is Knox going to be my new dad?

The pain almost buckles my knees.

Dammit. This is why I don't do these things. This is why I keep my distance. Feelings get involved and things invariably go wrong and—

"Did you see my goal?" His eyes are hopeful and his question…

It doesn't help the pain riddling my insides.

Tear the Band-aid.

But I can't seem to manage to as I whisper, "Yes." A beat. "And Evie did too." Despite myself, I feel my mouth curving. "She says it was the bestest goal she's ever seen."

He touches the backs of his knuckles to my cheek. God, I love it when he does that, love it even more when he steps closer, filling my nose with his scent, prickling my nerves, sending arousal blooming in my belly, and he smiles. "Prime compliments from a true hockey fan."

I laugh lightly. "Don't get too cocky. She also said it would be *so much better* if the puck was covered in sparkles."

His laughter fills the halls and it's fucking intoxicating.

Part of me just wants to stand here in bask in it or maybe fist pump and declare that *I* did that. That *I* made him laugh.

The rest knows…

I've already allowed myself to slip too far.

"Let's grab Winter," I say, stepping away from his touch. "I have a busy afternoon before I have to get Evie."

That amusement, the beautiful golden cloud of his humor—it's tempting to continue to bask in it. But I know the score, know where I'll end up, and—

No more.

Slowly, his hand drops to his side. "Did something happen while I was gone?"

"No," I say, brushing by him. "Why?"

A long blip of quiet before he speaks again. "No reason."

Oddly disappointed that he's letting it go—and chastising myself because I know I have absolutely no right to be—I move into Evie's room.

The furry pair look up at me, Winter's tail wagging and Snowball's eyes filled with annoyance. Something that disappears a moment later as Knox comes in behind me, Winter's tail shifting to hyperdrive.

"Hey, baby," he murmurs, bending down and scooping her up. She goes crazy licking his chin, trying to all but crawl into his skin. Even Snowball gets into the action, jumping onto her hind legs and resting her front paws against his leg.

And then she's also in Knox's arms, cradled by his gentle touch, his soft words.

And I'm on the outside.

My stomach twists, and I hate that I feel like I've just lost something important. I know this is the right move. Keep it cordial. Keep it simple.

No one gets hurt.

Right.

I slip from the room, pick up the bag and Winter's crate from the kitchen, and slip out the front door. Knox's car is unlocked, thankfully, so I tuck the items in the trunk and then turn for the house again to find him standing on the porch.

"What the fuck, lioness?" he asks quietly as he shuts the door behind him.

Winter's still in his arms, looking as contented as ever. Snowball likely got tired of scratches and returned to her sunny spot.

Am I jealous of the pooch? Yup.

Am I going to do anything about it? *Nope.*

"I'll let you get back to your day—" I begin.

"I say again," he growls, his eyes clashing with mine. "What the fuck is going on? I left here with a hot kiss and a hard-on, and I came back to..." He waves a hand.

"To what?"

"You icing me out."

I want to deny it. But I don't. For one, I can't. I *am* icing him out. For another, I *have* to ice him out.

Because if I don't—

Slip. Slip. *Slide.*

"Look," I begin. "We had a nice time—"

His brows shoot up and I hate the emotions that crawl across his expression—bewilderment and frustration and...

Hurt.

Better him than me.

Except, those words feel wrong—so damned wrong.

"Okay, so we had a great time," I blurt. "But neither of us are looking for a relationship, remember? This was a fun interlude and I'm happy to help out with Winter when you need, but that's all—"

I watch as his face locks down.

And I fucking hate it.

But I don't do anything to change it.

"I've got a pet sitter lined up," he says quietly.

I blink. "What?"

"I have a pet sitter lined up already," he semi-repeats as he brushes by me and tugs open his car door. I follow, watching as he settles Winter into some sort of car seat contraption for a dog that even comes with a seat belt he clips to her harness. He backs out, slams the door. "So don't worry about it. Winter's covered."

"Oh. Well, I—"

He tugs open the driver's side door, seeming to pluck the thoughts from my mind. "If Evie wants to see Winter, tell her I'll bring her to the rink some time."

"I—"

He swings the metal panel shut before I get the chance to finish the sentence.

And then he's turning on the engine, backing down the driveway.

And *then*...

He's gone.

Which is exactly what I wanted.

Right?

CHAPTER TWENTY-THREE

Knox

"So," Lake says as drops onto the bench. "What gives?"

I scowl and ignore him, ripping my jersey over my head and tossing it into the bin in the middle of the room, then start in on my other gear.

The game went fine.

Another night. Another game.

But I'm not fucking happy.

As great as the Vipers game had been, as much of a super-hero as I'd felt that night...

Today, there had been none of that.

It was a grind, a job, and nothing more.

I wasn't thinking about Evie watching after dance, wasn't trying to impress Ivy with my strength and speed.

It was all, grit my teeth, keep my head down, and drag myself through.

"He fucked it," Riggs mutters from my other side, dropping down next to me and getting to work on his own gear.

"Yup," Leo says from beside *him*. "Kid finally got over being gun shy and he fucked it."

A bolt of pain shoots through my jaw—too much teeth gritting tonight and not enough controlling my temper means that I'll likely be paying my dentist overtime. Especially since playing it cool and focused and calm seems very far away at the moment.

"Definitely fucked it," Lake agrees. "Man was looking for a fight all night—"

He's not lying. I *was* looking for a fight.

Unfortunately, no one from the other team was stupid enough to fuck around with me and give me one.

My own teammates on the other hand...

No. No punching the guys on the roster, especially the small subset I call my friends.

"I think maybe Knox has had enough for tonight," Storm says quietly as he yanks at the Velcro holding his shin guards in place.

Lake's brows lift and he makes a show of leaning around me, making eyes at Leo and Riggs. "That kid doesn't get it, does he?"

I roll my eyes, get to work tearing off my skates. "*That* kid is the only one who has my back," I grind out. "The rest of you fuckers just want to give me a hard time."

Leo's mouth twitches. "He's not wrong."

Lake chuckles. "What happened? The Knox Adler special brand of charm backfired?"

"No," I mutter.

Riggs sighs. "None of that shit that Ella said stuck, did it?"

Growling, I turn and slam my hand into his chest, gripping the cuff of his shoulder pads. "It stuck all right," I snap before I remember where the fuck I am and that I don't want the assholes on the other side of the room to clue in.

These assholes I call friends have my best interests in mind.

Those fuckers would love to have something more to give me shit about aside from my ability to work door handles.

And anyway, I'm pissed and hurt, but I don't want Ivy in their crosshairs.

She has enough shit to worry about, what with the asshole kid and the fucking principal and—

Me.

"I made my move," I say quietly, holding Riggs's eyes then glancing at Leo and Lake and Storm. "She just made it clear that she didn't want any part of *me*."

The silence that falls between us is full of shock.

And even though I'm fucking miserable, the fact that my friends are shocked loosens some of that knot in my stomach.

Of course, I suppose saying I *made my move* is a bit strong.

Yes, I went there with the *intention* of making my move, and I *did* try to get through to her.

She just made it clear that nothing else I said was going to make a difference.

So, why do I still feel like a coward?

I yank at my skate laces as laughter echoes across the room and I hear snippets of the conversation a couple of my teammates are having. "...never had a mouth like hers before. Bitch could take all of me and still want more."

"Not a problem when you've got a small dick," Lake mutters from next to me. He bumps his shoulder against mine, nods at the jackass crowing about his sexual prowess, and I take my first full breath for hours.

Yeah, I'm a little bitch, but I'm relieved that none of my friends are going to push this further.

Leo laughs and Riggs chuckles. Storm's mouth twitches and I nod my thanks at him.

Of course, all he gives me in return is a shrug.

Loquacious, he is not.

"Beers?" Lake asked.

I shake my head, adding before they can dig into me and my misery further, "Winter's at home alone. I need to make sure she's settled in. After our next home game, I'll buy."

Lake's stare holds mine for a long time.

Then he nods. "Bring the pup to the next Game Night. Steve needs a friend."

"You mean the demon dog known as Steve the pug needs to corrupt my innocent little pup?"

Lake snorts, but his expression isn't guilty in the least. "Damn right, he does. Nothing good ever comes from following the rules all the time."

"Swear to fuck that you stole *my* line," I grumble, shoving down my jock and wrapping a towel around my waist.

"Does sound like something an Adler would say," he agrees.

I roll my eyes.

"Which, of course," he goes on lazily, leaning back in his stall, "begs the question."

I shouldn't bite.

I *really* shouldn't bite.

But fucking curiosity killed the Adler.

"*What* question?" I ask between gritted teeth.

"Why you—as a pesky, boundary pushing, never met a challenge you didn't love to stick your nose in (and solve) Adler—gave up on something you want with only the barest *hint* of a fight."

And, with that, he claps me on the shoulder and stands, striding naked into the showers, giving the entire room the absolute certainty that not even Callie, with her talented mouth, would be able to handle all of him.

I know he's right.

I *didn't* fight.

Hell, I didn't even bicker.

And I certainly didn't abide by Ella's advice, even though it would be so much more convenient to believe that I had—

So much *safer* to pretend I had.

Be brave.

Yeah, I'd faced one wall—albeit a thick one topped with barbed wire, but one wall nonetheless—and I'd noped the fuck right out of there.

If anyone deserves someone to show her—and Evie—how beautiful love can be it's Ivy.

I knew walls were incoming and—

I'm a chicken shit.

My temple begins to throb again and the ache doesn't go away as I shower and get dressed.

It accompanies me to my car and all along my drive home.

It stays with me as I check on Winter and give in to those soft brown eyes, settling her on the pillow next to me.

That pain even clings to my dreams.

Probably because, for a second there, I actually thought I might be able to *live* them.

CHAPTER TWENTY-FOUR

Ivy

THE LAST THING I want to be doing the following week is going to the Sierra's charity event.

But I'm cramming my feet into heels and tugging up my zipper regardless.

"How do I look, Mom?" Evie asks as she sweeps into my room and does a twirl, fanning out the sparkly—of course—skirt of her dress.

"Beautiful, baby!" I tell her, leaning down and fussing with the strand of her hair I can never seem to get to cooperate. It always slips free of every hairstyle, no matter how many YouTube videos I watch or gallons of hairspray I use.

"You look beautiful too, Mom."

I smile. The love I have for my daughter—God, it's so strong it feels like I can't breathe sometimes.

"Thanks, honey," I say, leaning over to kiss the top of her head. "You ready to go?"

She nods.

"Great, can you get your jacket on and I'll be right behind you?"

Another nod, and this one sends more strands of her hair flying. Oy. I'm hopeless when it comes to braids.

At least Evie doesn't seem to notice as she skips off for the front door, her dress bouncing with every step.

Sighing, I look in the mirror and know this is as good as it gets—my hair in a low pony (I'm an expert at ponytails, low, mid, *or* high—it's just the braids that really trip me up. My simple sleeveless black jumpsuit and heels are topped off with a stack of bracelets on my left wrist and a pair of colorful plastic bead adorned earrings that Evie made for me in preschool.

"Good enough," I whisper.

Then I join Evie in the front room. I tug my coat off the hook and shrug into it, fix the tangle she's made of the sleeves of hers and all but wrestle her into it as she bounces with excitement and peppers me with questions.

"Is Ella going to be there?"

I nod, straighten out her hood. "Yes," I say. "Riggs told me that she's coming after work, along with Nova."

"Nova!" Evie dances around, scooping up Snowball and cuddling her against her chest as she spins around and around. "I love Nova!"

"I know you do. So"—I nudge her toward the door with a smile—"should we go and see her?"

"Yup!" She carefully sets Snowball onto her cat tower before bouncing her way out the door.

I follow her but don't make it all the way out before she tosses over her shoulder—

"And Knox?"

Guilt and longing slide through me and I struggle to keep my tone upbeat. "Of course, honey." Then I shut and lock the door, and bustle her over to the car, watching as she buckles herself in before I climb into the driver's seat.

But the flurry of activity doesn't distract her.

"When is Knox coming over with Winter again?"

"I don't know," I tell her as I navigate out onto the street. "He's been pretty busy with the season and I know he's been trying to get Winter settled at home and with his pet sitter."

Loaded silence from the back seat.

And disappointment in her eyes when our gazes connect in the rearview.

It's the disappointment that has me digging this hole deeper, has me blurting, "But he said you can visit Winter. He even promised to bring her to the rink soon."

"Really?"

The excitement back, and God, I'm reprehensible. But I still say, "*Really* really."

"Can I bring Snowball?"

"Not to the rink."

More disappointment.

"But if you visit at his house maybe." Digging. Digging. Digging that hole.

"Yes!"

"That's not a for sure, sweetheart. That's a maybe," I say, even though I know it likely won't be a problem—*if* he lets me in the front door. "Still, we can sure ask."

"Yay!" She wiggles in her booster, doing a happy dance then spends the next five minutes talking about how cute Winter is before pivoting to Ms. Phillips and music class and the art project she's working on, and then, "I saw James on the playground today—"

My stomach twists and I grip the steering wheel until it feels as though my hands are going to cramp.

Thankfully, her next words calm me.

"He was playing with a couple of my friends and they said he was nice."

My brows lift. "How was he nice?"

"He took turns in Wall Ball instead of getting mad and throwing the ball over the fence."

"Was there a grownup with him?" I ask when I pull to a stop at a red light.

"Yup," she says matter-of-factly. "Ms. Angie is his special friend and he doesn't go anywhere without her now." She turns her gaze out the window, watching the lights flash by as I start driving forward again. "'cept the bathroom."

I grin.

That's probably for the best.

"And what are you doing at recess?" My initial worry has receded but that doesn't mean I'm not going to keep a close eye on her.

"Lots of things."

"Like what?"

"We did hopscotch and the monkey bars and today Rylie and I did the twisty slide *five* times."

"Whoa," I say appreciatively. "That many?"

"And then we..."

The rest of the drive is filled with chatter about Rylie and the new dance routine Evie's learning in class and by the time we've parked and are walking into the building for the team event—this one being themed as Dress to the Nines—my daughter still hasn't run out of things to talk about.

Thankfully, my ears get a rest as she runs off to join a gaggle of girls all comparing sparkly dresses. I grin when I turn the corner and see the boys—and more than a few girls— playing knee hockey, more than a few of them in jerseys with the number nine on the back.

Dress to the *nines*—I appreciate the hustle.

Heh.

A few are sporting miniature suits that are freaking adorable, and there are more sparkly dresses and shiny patent leather shoes.

The staff, guys, and significant others are just as varied—though most have gone full formal wear as they stand around drinking and munching on snacks from the stations dotted around the room.

God, I hate this.

I sidestep a group of social media interns happily downing the free champagne and snacks and circle around to the food, filling a plate with the one good thing so far about tonight—a salad of spinach and strawberries and candied almonds with the yummiest raspberry vinaigrette I've ever tasted.

And then I take up my usual position at these things—propping up a wall, enjoying my salad, keeping an eye out for Evie, and...

Fading into the background.

Showing my face, checking that required box, and then getting the fuck out.

Evie runs up to me a while later, skidding to a halt mere inches before slamming into me. Her cheeks are red and her braid is all but falling out, and I sigh—I really *am* hopeless when it comes to braids. "Ella said she'll fix my hair, is that okay?"

"Honey," I begin. "I'm sure Ella doesn't want to work tonight—"

The look on her face—

God, why do I love this girl so much?

"I don't mind," I hear from my left before I can push through the Mom Guilt and tell my daughter to not bother Ella.

"I—"

Ella settles a hand on my arm. "I just didn't want to ruin your handiwork."

Laughter bubbles up in my chest. "As you can see, braiding isn't my strong suit."

Ella's lips twitch. "Nah," she says. "It just can't stand up to the power that's Evie, muahaha!"

I chuckle as Evie strikes a superhero (or maybe it's a villain) pose, and then I watch closely, trying to absorb the knowledge and a modicum of Ella's skills as she pulls a brush from her purse and gets to work on Evie's hair.

But I know it's hopeless as her hands work far faster than I can track, and in less than five minutes she has Evie's hair tamed into a beautiful braid that circles the crown of her head.

"I don't have any glitter tonight," Ella says as she tucks the brush away. "But I do have…" With a flourish she pulls out a velvet ribbon that works perfectly with Evie's dress and ties it into a bow.

"What do you think, Mom?" Evie asks when she's done.

"Beautiful," I say softly.

The bow. Her hair. My daughter's smile. Sharing this moment with her.

Ella bumps her shoulder against mine. "She's wonderful."

"So are you," I say as Evie runs off.

"Pish."

"Thanks," I whisper, my heart squeezing as I watch her.

"Anytime," she whispers back and we stand there for a moment before she turns to face me. "I wanted to ask you if—"

"Ella!"

A band of hockey players appears.

"Hey, guys," she says. "I just need to—"

But before she can finish that or what she wanted to ask me, she's bustled off.

"I'll find you later," she calls to me as Riggs all but drags her away.

I smile and wave…and go back to my propping up the wall. I finish my salad, have a single glass of champagne (because free champagne), and I'm about to go and track down Evie when my daughter skids to a stop in front of me again.

"Almost ready to go, pumpkin?"

"Can I have a sleepover with Blake?" she asks without preamble.

Blake being the daughter who belongs to the team's doctor. *Blake* being a precocious little girl I had over for a sleepover a few weeks ago.

Blake also being the sweet-faced little girl currently standing arm-in-arm with my daughter—both of whom are staring at me with pleading expressions.

But it's Friday night.

I don't have work tomorrow and I *really* don't want to go back to an empty house tonight and—

"Is that okay?" I look up into the eyes of Dr. Haley Montgomery.

"Is it okay with you guys?" I say. "I know you've only just gotten back into town."

Her mouth curves up. "Honestly?" A flick of her gaze at the pair. "They'll keep each other busy and give John"—her husband—"and I some time to catch up."

And how can I deny her that?

"It's okay with me," I say. "I'll drop off a bag of clothes and her toothbrush and stuff."

Haley waves me off. "We have extra toothbrushes and she can borrow some of Blake's things. You take the night off from Mom Duties and just enjoy the break."

God, no.

I need to keep busy.

Need the distraction.

But I just slap a smile on my face and thank her before I bend down to hug Evie and remind her to be on her best behavior...

Then I'm watching the girls skip away, Haley and John trailing them and...

I'm alone.

In a room full of people.

And even though I haven't allowed myself to go there all night, without the distraction of Evie all of a sudden I'm in the deep end, drinking in the sight of...

Knox.

He's so fucking gorgeous—tall and strong and smiling wide. He's surrounded by his teammates, looking like he's having the time of his life.

And I'm here feeling...

Things.

Suddenly, my lungs are tight and my feet are pinching and my jumpsuit is too tight.

I set my glass down, slip out into the dark hallway, and round the corner, needing the shadows and the quiet and a moment of solitude to pull my shit together.

I made this choice.

I ended it before I got in too deep—or so I'd thought.

Or so I'd *hoped.*

"Fucking delusional," I whisper, dropping my chin to my chest and exhaling slowly.

When the tightness in my throat fades and my eyes stop burning, I lift my head.

Go home.

Forget about Kn—

But I don't get to finish the thought.

Because it's at that precise moment I realize I'm not alone.

CHAPTER TWENTY-FIVE

Knox

I FROWN when Ivy doesn't come back.

I've been watching her all night, trying not, knowing it's stupid to be memorizing every beautiful part of her—the hot as fuck outfit, those spiked heels, the sparkling jewelry, the makeup that's heavier than normal. The way she eats with abandon but carefully sips one glass of champagne. The softness in her face as she watches out for Evie as she plays, the gratitude in her eyes when Ella does her hair magic.

I'm fucking obsessed.

I'm tired of fighting it.

And...Lake's right. I didn't do enough, didn't say enough, didn't make my feelings clear.

I need her to know everything. I need to show her how I feel.

If after that she decides—

My lungs tighten.

Then tighten further when I realize...she still hasn't come back from the hall.

It's probably nothing.

Only...my fucking spidey senses are tingling

She's been gone far too long now to just be using the bathroom. Unless she's not feeling well. Or she slipped in those sky high heels and hurt herself. Or—

Laughter echoes from the circle of people surrounding me, everyone enjoying some punchline I was too busy worrying to actually listen to.

"And then," Leo says, drawing Jolie into his side, "I told her she can either shape up or ship out—"

Jolie swats him on the chest. "You did not!" Her eyes lift from his, locking on each of ours in turn. "Because otherwise *he'd* be the one being shipped out."

The circle laughs and I take that moment to slip away. "Getting a drink," I lie when Ella's gaze comes to mine.

She opens her mouth, closes it, then nods and leans heavier into Riggs's side.

I'll take it.

I go to one of the tables, snagging a beer for appearances sake, but instead of going back to my friends, I make a slow circuit of the room, seeing if I somehow missed Ivy coming back in.

Not likely considering how closely I've tracked her...

But there *are* multiple entrances and exits.

It's possible.

Except, when I make that circle, when I study every shadowy corner and alcove...she's not anywhere in the room.

And the longer she's out of sight, the more my spidey senses tingle and the tighter the knot that's my insides grows.

"Fuck," I mutter quietly as I step out into the hall.

I check the women's bathroom, poking my head in, heart sinking when it's empty, then stop by the men's, just for good measure, but aside from one of my teammate's taking a piss, that's empty too.

I push out through the door, look left and right down the

hallway, and I'm just about to head back into the main room when I hear a noise.

A grunt? Or a sharp exhale?

"What the fuck?" I whisper, alarm bells blaring. I cock my head and strain to listen.

And that's when I hear it again, sharper this time.

Not a grunt.

It's a cry—of pain, of fear, of…

Fuck it. It doesn't matter *what* the noise is. I just know it's bad, so I take off running, sprinting for the end of the hall and when I turn the corner and the shadows materialize into….*people*…I pause.

And then I see red.

No, it's far past red.

It's Ivy, pinned against the wall by…

"Coach?" I whisper incredulously at the same time she shoves him back.

"No!" she cries out, and one look at her face tells me that whatever the fuck has been happening isn't welcome.

I react before I really process moving, grabbing the back of Coach's suit jacket and ripping him away from her. He stutters out a breath and fuck, but he smells like a distillery—swear to God I'm getting drunk contact just by inhaling.

"Yes," Coach mutters, barely processing that I'm dragging him back, that I'm *tossing* him back, all but throwing him against the opposite wall.

He hits with a *thunk* that probably isn't good, but I don't give a fuck about him right now.

Not when Ivy is looking…

Like *that*.

"Lioness," I say softly.

She jerks, wild, terrified eyes coming to mine. "I didn't— He —" She's trembling, palms pressed into the wall, nails scrabbling against the surface, as though trying, and unable, to find purchase. "I didn't want—"

"I know," I tell her. "I *know*."

I hear movement behind me, but when I whip around, prepared to punch the fuck out of the man who, quite literally, holds my career in his hands, it's to find the drunk fucker sliding to the floor, as though his legs can't hold him up any longer.

I've heard that Coach can tie one on with the best of them, I've even seen him buzzed a handful of times—

But this?

No. No fucking *way*.

I want to plow my fist into his drunk face, to do it again and again until he's reduced to bloody pulp.

But Ivy is more important.

"Are you hurt?" I ask quietly.

She jerks and, fuck, I want to pull her against me, want to hold her close, but she's not ready for that. "No," she whispers, palms pushing off the wall. She crosses her arms over her chest, as though holding herself together. "No, he didn't hurt me."

Except, I can see fingerprints on her arms...

On her fucking *throat*.

I'm going to kill him.

"Ivy, baby," I say carefully. "I'm going to touch you." I need to make sure she's not hurt anywhere else, that she's not concussed.

She shakes her head, hard just once. "No," she says. "I'm fine. I'm totally fine."

That's *totally* bullshit.

"Give me your hand, lioness," I murmur. "Please?"

Her throat works and I think she's going to refuse. But after a long moment, she drops her hand into mine.

Carefully, *slowly* I draw her into my arms, gently prodding at her skull. When I find it free of bumps, I bring her closer, hating that she's trembling, hating more when her words come fast and furious and filled with terror.

"I-it's not a big deal," she says. "H-he g-gets like this s-sometimes. When he's drunk. Usually I can distract him, get him yelling a-about hockey so he d-doesn't—" Her chest expands on a shuddering breath. "S-so he doesn't do this."

All I'm hearing is that he's done this before.

And now I *really* want to commit murder.

"What the fuck?"

Ivy jumps and I settle one hand on her nape turning us so my body shields her. I glance over my shoulder at Lake, who's come around the corner, taken one look at the situation, and knows exactly what the fuck is happening.

"Get Damon," I say quietly, knowing that the team's general manager is here tonight and needs to come handle this shit.

Ivy jerks in my hold again. "N-no," she says, trying to push away from me. "I'm fine. It's all fine. R-really."

Lake just meets my eyes and nods.

"I need a drink!" Coach hollers, trying to push up to his feet, but Lake didn't come alone, I realize. Riggs is here. And Leo and Storm.

And Ella and Nova.

Good to have witnesses.

Bad because this is going to kill Ivy.

I turn to my sister. "Get her coat and purse?"

Ella's eyes drift down to Ivy pressed against my chest. Then she nods, threading her arm through Nova's and drawing her away.

"Kn-Knox," Ivy says when they've gone, pushing lightly against my chest, her trembling easing. "We shouldn't make a b-big deal about this. I'm f-fine and—"

I cup her jaw, tilt her head up so that our stares are aligned. "We're making a big deal about this. Because it *isn't* fine."

"I—" Her eyes are damp and she presses her lips together.

"It. *Isn't*. Fine."

Her lids slide closed, a tear skating down her cheek.

I wipe it off, bend down so I can whisper in her ear. "And it isn't your fault."

Another jerk, but because this one is paired with a hitch in her breathing, with more tears escaping, I don't say anything else.

I just hold her as she quietly cries.

And I don't let go, not when Lake comes back with Damon and not when…

All hell breaks loose.

CHAPTER TWENTY-SIX

Ivy

THIS IS MY NIGHTMARE.

My literal fucking *nightmare.*

Not only do I have bruises on my arms, my throat from Hiller's drunken proposition—

No.

I'm lying to myself.

It was more than a *proposition,* and I hate the knot in my stomach, the one that reminds me how much worse it could have been if Knox hadn't come across us when he did.

Just as much as I hate the soreness in my throat from Hiller's unhappiness at my answer.

Thank God Evie wasn't there.

Thank God she won't be home until tomorrow, so I have time to get my shit together.

I close my eyes, squeezing the lids so tightly together that not a sliver of light sneaks in.

And I stay that way for the entire drive home.

Until there's a hand on my arm and I turn to look at Ella. "We're home," she whispers.

Nodding jerkily, I reach for the handle and pop open the door. "Thanks for the ride," I say, glancing around for my purse, not even realizing that Nova's in the back seat until she opens her door and I see she's holding it.

"We'll just get you settled inside," she says quietly.

Quietly but *firmly*.

And I'm too tired to argue.

"Okay," I murmur and close the door, start up the walkway, my heels clicking on the concrete. She passes me my purse when I get there and I dig out my keys, my hands shaking as I lift them to the lock.

"I've got it," Ella murmurs, carefully reaching forward, slipping the keys from my hold and unlocking the door.

And then we're walking into the house.

I drop my purse on the table, hear Ella set my keys beside it, and then Nova is moving by me and into the kitchen. There's the sound of the fridge opening and closing, a rattle in my cupboards, the *click click click* of the range turning on.

"Come on," Ella says, gently slipping her arm around my waist and drawing me down the hall. "Let's get you into something more comfortable."

"I'm fine."

"I know you are," she says, pausing to peek into Evie's room, the bathroom, and then finally flicking on the lights in my room.

I blink against the sudden brightness and then again when Ella slips by me, goes to my dresser and starts pulling out clothes—my softest sweats, a pair of fuzzy socks, a loose tee, and a thick sweatshirt.

I don't even realize I'm cold until I see them.

"Change," she orders softly. "I'll wait in the hall."

And then she's walking from my room, quietly closing the door behind her.

I stand there, just shivering, for a long moment, but eventually I snap out of it, fingers finding the tab of the underarm zipper, dragging it down. I kick off my heels, shove off my jumpsuit and underwear, unclip my bra and throw them all into a crumpled pile in the corner of the room. I drag the tee and sweatshirt over my head, don the socks and sweats and then...

I drop my chin to my chest and try to breathe, hating that this happened, hating myself because I thought I was delusional enough to avoid it, hating that I probably won't have a job with the team for much longer, that Evie will lose something else because I couldn't keep it together.

Hating that Knox was there, that Leo and Lake and Riggs were too. That Ella and Nova were so quiet in the car on the way here, that they seem to know precisely how fragile I feel right now—

Hiller being hauled to his feet and dragged away.

The police showing up and talking to everyone, including me.

Being shown to an empty room and having pictures taken.

Damon Connors staring at me with cold eyes.

A quiet knock startles me out of my head.

"Need some help?" Ella calls through the door.

"I'm fine," I say, pulling it open. "Thanks," I add when her gaze skates over me from head to toe. "I feel a lot better now. You guys can—"

She weaves her arm through mine, guides me into the kitchen.

Nova has three mugs on the counter and she picks one up, walks over to us. "Something to warm you up."

"You didn't have—"

She cuts me off with a small shake of her head. "I know. But I —we—wanted to. And sometimes..." Her eyes are sad and I know she and Ella both have experienced dark stuff too.

And I hate it.

"Sometimes," she says again, "it's nice to be warm and safe and to self-medicate with a delicious mug of hot chocolate."

My lips twitch.

And somehow, *somehow*, I'm smiling.

"Not sure my nutrition training talked about the medicinal properties of chocolate."

Ella bumps her shoulder against mine and I glance over, see that Snowball's claimed her and is currently rubbing her adorable face against Ella's throat. "Then your education is clearly lacking." She kisses Snowball's head. "There are two truths in life—Nova's hot chocolate always makes things better—"

"*And* my honey rosemary Moscow mules," Nova says with a wink.

"And her mules," Ella amends, setting Snowball down when she starts squirming.

"What's the other truth?" I ask, accepting the mug that Nova passes over.

Blue eyes, so much like Knox's, fix on mine, and her voice is quiet when she murmurs, "That there's nothing scarier than falling in love."

"Word," Nova mutters, turning back to the counter and retrieving the other mugs.

I lift the cup to my lips, take a big sip. It's to avoid responding to that statement, to prevent myself from thinking about it...and how they may be true, but the moment the drink hits my tongue, my taste buds explode in happiness.

Ella grins as Nova hands her a mug. "Been convinced about the medicinal properties yet?"

I take another sip. "I'm considering it."

Nova giggles. "Me too," she says. "And it might take me a whole 'nother mug to get there."

I laugh—

And that's the moment I see movement out of the corner of my eye.

CHAPTER TWENTY-SEVEN

Knox

I've been bracing myself the entire drive over—

But I never could have predicted that I would walk into this.

Ivy laughing.

Riggs exhales from beside me, whispers reverently, "My cherié." And as though Ella hears him, her head comes up and expression is so beautiful, it's almost painful.

She sets her mug on the island, glances at Nova.

But Nova's already sensed that we're here—or that Lake is, anyway. She puts her mug down too, leans close to Ivy, and says something I can't hear.

Ivy nods, her back going stiff, and after an extended moment, she sets her own cup down and rotates to face us.

Bracing.

Putting those shields back into place.

Hiding.

Well, I'm not going away this time, not going to be a fucking chicken shit again and let her push me away. Not after the way we danced around each other the last week, not after the stolen moments together the week before that mean everything, not after her gaze barely left me all night, not after—

Fucking *Hiller*.

Luckily, I brought my shield buster.

"Woof!"

I set Winter onto the floor, and the way the pup is able to navigate with the cast is commendable, the same as she somehow knows to go straight to Ivy.

"Call us if you need anything," Lake says.

I nod and then follow them as they finish their goodbyes, gather up their belongings, and slip out the front door. I flick the lock behind them then go back into the kitchen.

Ivy's sitting on the floor Winter in her lap, Snowball curled up at her side.

Right.

This isn't going to work.

I cross over to her, bend down, and scoop her, Winter, and Snowball up.

"What—?"

But I don't stop, just straighten and carry the trio down the hall, and settle them gently on the bed.

Winter's nonplussed, just happy to be close to Snowball and Ivy. The cat, on the other hand, glares at me for daring to change her position, though she tolerates the apologetic scratch I give her beneath her chin.

I get another glare, though, when I toe off my shoes and climb in behind them.

And it's not from Snowball.

"I don't know why everyone's making a big deal," Ivy says. "I'm fine. I just need a good night's sleep and I'll be good to go in the morning."

"I might believe that if you weren't still shaking."

She inhales sharply. "I'm—"

My temper begins to fray. "If you say you're *fine*, swear to fuck I'll..." I trail off because I don't have a suitable threat.

THE BIG SKATE 157

And she knows it.

"You'll what?" she prods.

I sigh, draw her a little more firmly against my chest. "Sic Winter"—I get a tail wag—"and all her kissing abilities on you."

Silence.

Long enough that the worry inside me begins to spread out again, begins to eat away at me, but then she laughs softly. "What if I like her kissing skills?"

"More than you like mine?"

"I—" She falls quiet and the moment stretches between us, taut and filled with far too many things that have been left unsaid.

"Sorry," I say, letting her off the hook. "This is not the time."

She exhales quietly. "I didn't handle the other day well. You're right to be pissed."

"I'm not pissed, lioness. Not at you, anyway," I add when she snorts.

"At Hiller?"

Like that's even a question.

"He hurt you, baby. He put his hands on you and scared you —" I pause, trying to decide if I'm going to push this. Then deciding that I *have* to. "And you made it seem like he's done it before."

She's still as a fucking statue for long enough that words bubble up in the back of my throat and I have to swallow them down.

"He made it clear that he'd welcome anything I would give him—willingly or not."

I clench my teeth together so tightly that a bolt of pain slices through my jaw. Christ. More dental work in my future. But I'm only thinking that, clinging to that tiny moment of levity so I don't get out of bed and punch something. "Did he hurt you before?"

"No," she whispers. "He just tried to break me down so I'd give in."

Rage in my belly. More pain through my jaw. "What does that mean?"

"You don't want to hear this."

"What does that mean?" I ask again, more firmly this time.

She groans softly. "Knox—"

"You might as well face it, lioness," I tell her. "I'm not leaving. Not now. Not tomorrow." Not ever, though I don't say the last out loud, not as the tension in her frame ratchets up with each word I speak.

"I—"

"Tell me," I order quietly.

A long-suffering sigh. "It means he would corner me in his office and threaten my job. It means that he'd proposition me and get handsy any time I was dumb enough to be alone with him. It means that he told me if I blew him he'd give me a raise."

I clamp my eyes closed, clench my jaw through that bolt of pain. "Anything else?"

Her throat works. "That's pretty much it."

Pretty much. Jesus Christ.

"Tell me the rest."

"Knox—"

"*Lioness.*"

"I went to HR once and he found out. Next time I showed up for a meeting, he passed me a folded piece of paper. It was my resignation letter." Her voice wobbles. "Said if I ever threw him under the bus again like that, I wouldn't have a job, would never work in the league again." She clears her throat and I watch her somehow piece herself together. "I didn't have enough private clients then. Things are different now. When Damon lets me go, I'll be ok—"

"What the fuck?" I catch her chin. "There is absolutely no fucking way that Damon would let you go for this—"

"HR—"

"Fuck HR. This happened at a company event, was witnessed by multiple players, and caught on camera—" She jerks, but I keep going. I *have* to make her understand. "There's a police report and we all saw those bruises on your body, baby."

"Oh God," she whispers.

"This isn't an email that is going to be hidden by bureaucracy. This is a major fuck up, and if anyone isn't going to work in the league again, it's going to be Hiller."

"You can't know that—"

I slip Winter from her arms, nudge Snowball from her lap. Then I carefully turn her to face me. Her expression is stricken, her skin pale, those fucking bruises standing out in sharp relief. "We all know it wasn't your fault," I say, cupping her cheeks. "And I know that Damon is going to do right by you, lioness."

"How?"

"His sister was raped, baby," I say gently. "Back when he was playing. It was big news because he found out, lost his shit, and beat the asshole to a pulp. The prison sentence for assault voided his contract."

"Oh, my God."

"He didn't play after that. But eventually he found a job in the back office and now—"

She swallows hard. "He's the GM."

I nod. "He can be an asshole and difficult to work with...but there's one thing that he won't ever tolerate."

I see it then.

Finally.

The relief creeping into her pretty brown eyes. "Coach Joey and him were talking when I left," I say. "I have no doubt that she'll be taking over and Hiller is gone."

Her chin drops to her chest, and she exhales. "Maybe I should be sad about him losing his job—"

"No, you shouldn't," I growl.

Her head pops up.

"No," I say again, more firmly.

The corners of her mouth soften, as though she's almost smiling. Then any hint of amusement is gone. "Knox"—she sighs and settles her hand on my chest, just above my heart—"about last week. I'm—"

I press a finger to her lips. "Don't worry about last week. We're here now and—"

"No," she says, peeling my finger free. "I need to explain. I —" Her eyes slam closed. "Evie asked if you were going to be her dad—"

I choke.

Those lids peel back, and the amusement returns in the form of a small smile. "Yeah," she says. "*Exactly.*"

"Baby, that's not what I meant."

Her brows flick up. "What *do* you mean?"

"I know you're a package deal and Evie is great." I just... well, I just accepted my feelings, just found the courage to put the bullshit in my head aside.

I hadn't gotten as far as *Dad.*

As though she can hear that thought, her lips twitch. "We are. But she asked and I made up some excuse to put her off and then when you showed up that day I'd convinced myself it couldn't work." I open my mouth and she waves a hand, continuing, "But you were in front of me and...I was feeling all of that— well, I was feeling all the *stuff* between us—the need, the desire, the way I'm always so aware of you, and...I panicked. I knew this couldn't end well. God, if I know anything about you, it's that you have no plans of settling down—"

"Had," I correct quietly.

A long, slow blink. "What?"

"I *had* no plans of settling down."

CHAPTER TWENTY-EIGHT

Ivy

I GAPE AT HIM, heart pounding. "What are you saying?"

"You know what I'm saying, lioness," he says. "I like you. I like Evie. You're smart and capable and beautiful and so damned strong. And Evie is amazing—she's bright and as smart as her mama"—he brushes his knuckles over my cheek—"and she has this huge heart that just sucks you in."

My eyes are stinging. "But you always push my buttons."

His mouth hitches up. "I'm an Adler, baby. I live to be annoying."

I laugh and it's a little watery.

Something he—*of freaking course*—notices, his hands shifting until he's cupping my jaw. "Spending time with you is…"

"What?" I ask.

He exhales, worry creeping back into his eyes. "If Evie's question had you pushing me away…"

My pulse picks up its pace. "Tell me," I whisper.

He studies me closely then exhales. "I've never felt more right, more at home than when I'm with you—not since my mom was alive."

"Knox. I'm sorry—"

A finger to my lips again. "It's not a happy story, lioness, though my early years were. But when I was in middle school, my mom unexpectedly got pregnant—her and my dad were thrilled, and we were excited too, but—"

My stomach twists.

"Things went wrong, and we lost both of them."

"Oh, my God. Honey, I—"

But I can't find the words and he keeps talking, filling in the rest of it. "It was traumatic for all of us. One second we were painting the nursery and the next we were calling 9-1-1 and watching our mom be loaded in the back of an ambulance. And —" He exhales. "She didn't come home."

Shit.

"Then things got worse."

"How?" I rasp out.

"My dad…he went off the deep end. He just stopped parenting, stopped engaging with us. It was like one day we went from being a happy family of four to the next it just being Ella and me. We felt like orphans. We felt *abandoned.* And then—"

"Oh, God," I whisper. "There's more?"

His smile is sad and totally *not* Knox-like. "Unfortunately, yes."

I take his hand, lace my fingers through his. "Lay it on me."

A little warmth in his smile—thank God. "The rest of it is typical shit—he remarried, made a new family, forgot about us further, and then it really *was* just Ells and me."

"I'm so sorry, Knox."

"Me too," he murmurs, running his thumb lightly along the back of my hand.

"Honey—"

"Here's the thing, lioness," he says. "It's the past and it sucks and I can't lie—I let it tear me to pieces for a long time. For *too* fucking long. It wasn't until I saw Lake and Leo find their people that allowing someone in my life in that way even became a consideration. But it wasn't until Ella fell for Riggs that I began to truly trust it. To *want* it. And it wasn't until you that I knew I had to have it."

My heart lurches in my chest, slamming itself against my rib cage over and over again.

"But I've been fighting my past."

"How?"

He exhales, hand tightening around mine. "How could I dare let myself have it?" he asks. "Everyone always said that I'm the spitting image of my dad, that I'm *just* like him—so how could I trust myself to make a family if I might freak out and fuck up like he did?"

"You wouldn't—"

"How can you know? How can *I* know?"

I hesitate because there *isn't* a way I can give him an answer and know it's absolutely, one hundred percent the right one. Life is lifey, things change, *people* change.

Bad things happen, despite the best of intentions.

And it's like he sees all of that ping-ponging around in my brain, and the look in his eyes—

Fuck, it hurts.

And it makes me say something I would have thought I needed to be under the pain of death to admit. "All I know is that I trust you."

The pain clouding the gorgeous blue gaze fades, replaced by—

Something I can't look too closely at.

So, I give as good as he gave me.

"Like your dad, my parents weren't great," I tell him. "And I spent years being shepherded around family members and in and out of the system. I just wanted a place that was permanent, somewhere there was absolutely no doubt that I belonged."

"And did you find it?"

My eyes sting. "No," I say quietly. "I'm still looking for it."

His hand settles on my nape. "Lioness," he murmurs. "I—"

"I have Evie," I tell him. "I'm not completely pathetic."

"Hey—"

"It's a joke," I say with a shrug. "A lame attempt at one," I add when he scowls. "My point is that Evie's always been my person, and even though I didn't pick a good man for her dad" —well, I didn't really choose him at all because he…well, he did much worse to me than Hiller ever did—"I think she and I have managed to build a pretty great life."

"It's a beautiful life," he whispers.

Damn. There go my eyes again.

And my heart.

"Yes," I agree. "It's a beautiful life. And"—here I pluck up my courage, release my grip of that slippery hillside and take the biggest leap of faith I've made in years—"I think we can have something even better." His face changes and I rush to add, "I don't know how long it'll last or if we'll be something close to forever, but…I know you well enough by now to understand that you'll never hurt me or Evie, and I've never had that before."

His eyes close. "Fuck," he whispers.

A sinking feeling in my stomach. "What?"

"Ella gave me a whole pep talk last week about taking the leap and being brave." He peels back his lids and relief courses through me at the amusement in his eyes. "And here you are just being my fearless lioness."

I don't feel brave, and my fear is roiling right beneath the surface, but I can hear the sincerity in his tone, see his belief of his words all throughout his face.

And…somehow they become one of the best things I've ever heard.

Right up there with all the naughty, wonderful things he'd told me while we were naked in this bed.

And Evie saying *Mama* for the first time.

"Why do you call me that?"

"Lioness?"

I nod.

"Because everyone knows that the lionesses are the true heart of the pride—they're smart, work hard, and run the show." He winks. "Kind of like someone else I know."

"Don't lions nap like twenty-two hours a day?"

His mouth quirks. "I just call that having great time management skills."

Laughter bubbles up in my chest.

He runs his knuckles over my cheek. "You're beautiful when you laugh."

My lungs hitch. "Knox."

"I like it better when you call me *honey*."

"*Knox.*"

He gives me that unrepentant smile that used to make me want to kiss and kill him in equal measure. Tonight, though, it just makes me want to kiss him.

But there's a part of me that needs him to know—

"You're not your dad."

His big chest expands and collapses on a breath, then he shifts, coaxing us onto our sides, my back tucked against his front, drawing the blankets over us and settling the animals when they protest.

An arm over my middle.

A strong body behind me.

Warm all around me.

"Yeah, lioness" he says long moments later, when my eyes have grown heavy and sleep is creeping in. "I'm starting to think that I'm not like him at all."

CHAPTER TWENTY-NINE

Knox

I EXHALE, the cool morning air creating a cloud of condensation around me as I supervise Winter in Ivy's back yard.

She's not in any hurry to do her business, apparently, considering she's spent the last ten minutes sniffing every rock and pine needle.

There's a creak, a whoosh of air, and I turn to see Ivy walking out onto the porch.

She's in those fuzzy pajamas, thick socks, and oversized sweatshirt, and she's still beautiful enough to take my breath away.

"Hey, lioness."

Her eyes are wary, but there's no sign of thick walls to keep me out, and I exhale again. "I wasn't sure how you take your coffee," she says quietly, holding up the mugs in her hands.

"Just black."

A twitch of her lips. "That's how you got all the hair on your chest?"

"You saying I'm some sort of Sasquatch or something?" I tease, accepting the mug she holds out.

"If the shoe—or maybe I should say, *skate*, fits." She drags her gaze down my front and every part of me snaps to rigid attention.

Every part.

In a way, it was hell sleeping beside her, holding her, and not doing more.

But in another, it was...perfect.

"You could certainly do with some manscaping—"

My mouth falls open and I set my mug on the railing, turn to face her. "Rude."

"I say again"—and fuck, but I love that she feels safe enough, comfortable enough to tease me—"if the skate fits."

"And *I* say again—" I snag the mug from her, set it beside mine on the railing, then snag her wrist and yank her against me. "*Rude.*"

"Knox," she whispers, snaking the arm that's now trapped between us up, up, *up*...until it's resting on my chest, just over my heart. She flexes her fingers, and my heart goes double time —something I know that she can feel because her expression softens and she whispers my name again.

I tuck a wayward strand of hair behind her ear. "How are you feeling today?"

She screws up her face, and I grin.

"That good, huh?"

She shrugs. "I've been better." A sigh. "And I've been worse."

"I hate that for you."

She touches my cheek. "I hate a lot of stuff." She steps closer. "For both of us."

"We're a pair, huh?"

A soft laugh, but she allows me to draw her closer, her body relaxing against mine.

All I know is that I trust you.

I tighten my hold then give her back her mug and jerk my chin out toward the yard. "Winter's happy."

"Lots of pine needles to sniff."

"And bushes."

"And rocks."

"Woof!"

She chuckles. "And shadows to bark at."

We fall silent, and I hold her as I watch the pooch, listen to the sounds of morning, feel the cool breeze on my skin.

"You cold?" I ask after we've stood there, watching Winter and sipping our coffees for a few minutes.

"No," she says. "But we can go inside if you are."

"I'm not cold." I smooth a hand down her back then lift my mug. "But I could use a top off."

"I can—"

"I'll get it, lioness." I nudge her toward one of the chairs. "Why don't you take a load off, and I'll get us both a refill."

"You don't have—"

I cup her jaw. "I think we've established by now that this—*us*—is something we both want."

Wide eyes, pink cheeks.

"Capisce?"

Her lips part on an inhale, then she exhales and nods. *"Capisce."* She holds up her mug. "One milk. Two sugars."

"Good." I snag her mug. "And got it." I turn for the house, chuckling when Winter follows me inside and promptly tries to climb up next to Snowball on the couch in the living room. I give her a boost, shake my head when they both sigh in contentment.

Those two.

Grinning, I top off our mugs, add Ivy's milk and sugar, then head back outside.

"We've been abandoned?" she asks lightly when I pass her the refilled mug.

"Yup. Winter decided the appeal of Snowball was too tempting to ignore."

Her lips twitch, and I settle into the chair next to her. We're doing something completely normal, something someone might even say is boring, but...I'm settled, content, *home*.

And an idiot to have ever run from this.

"I didn't thank you for last night."

I bump my knee against hers. "Pretty sure you did."

She shakes her head. "No, I didn't."

"Ivy, I told you. I don't need—"

One second, she's sitting next to me, the next her mug is on the deck and she's plucking mine from my hands. She sets it down and turns to me.

"Lioness?" I ask, lifting my eyebrows.

She clambers onto my lap. "Yeah?"

"Wanna clue me in?"

She cups my cheeks, holds my gaze. "You're wonderful, Knox Adler."

I inhale sharply. "Baby—"

"Shh," she says lazily, dragging a finger down my chest, dipping it beneath the waistband of my sweats.

One brush along the head of my cock and I'm hard.

"Baby," I begin again.

"Hush," she says, gripping me, stroking me firmly. "No more darkness. No more past. We're here together and alone and…I want you."

If I was hard before…

Now I can barely think because there's no blood left in my brain.

But one thing penetrates.

"I don't have a condom," I blurt, needing to make that clear before things go too far, before my control unravels any further—

But she doesn't help my control because she just reaches into the pocket of her sweatshirt and grins, pulling out the small foil square with a flourish. "But I do."

And then she yanks at the waistband of my pants, dragging them and my underwear down enough for my cock to pop out.

"Like my own personal present," she says, fisting me, leaning forward, and sucking me cock deep in one slick movement.

"*Fuck*," I growl as she seals her mouth over me. "Lioness, I—"

One touch.

One stroke.

One hot, wet mouth...

And I'm dangerously close, even before she starts working me in tandem, mouth and fist, lips and teeth, tongue and—

I jerk. "Christ, lioness!"

"Just making sure you're paying attention."

I'm paying attention. An earthquake could be shattering the world around us and my focus would still be reduced to her and only her.

As she sucks and strokes.

As she takes me so deep her eyes fill with tears and cling to those thick lashes.

As she moans and works me faster.

Harder.

Until I lose patience and...

Drag her off me.

"My turn," I growl as I reach for her.

But she backs away from me, tosses the condom into my lap and stands.

"Lioness—"

Her answer is pushing down and stepping out of her sweats, her underwear. Then she turns away from me, and...

Bends over the railing.

That lush ass, her strong thighs and calves, the scorching hot look she tosses me over her shoulder.

Control?

What the fuck is that?

Cursing softly, I struggle to think, to slow down. I want to plunge deep inside her, fuck her hard and fast and furious, but...

Control.

My head spins, and frankly, it's miracle that I'm conscious at this point at all, considering all the blood in my body is currently pooling in my cock, but I am and I take advantage of it, rolling the condom down then standing and moving to her, kicking her feet apart.

"Knox—*oh, God.*"

Okay, maybe thrusting into her in one smooth stroke isn't exactly *control*, but her pussy clamping around me tells me she likes it. The same as her head dropping back and her hips moving against me, and—

Her moan.

It's beautiful, that moan, her body, the tight clasp of her cunt, and I tell her, knowing she likes the words, knowing that she likes me telling her how wet she is, how good she feels, how much I want her.

I feel it in the ripples of her pussy, the arch of her spine, the way her hips grind back against me.

I feel it in the shudders of her body, the deepening of her groans, her pelvis jerking, seeking out more and more and *more* of me.

And with each stroke, I give it to her.

Give her *all* of me.

Until she stills and—

"Knox!"

Until she's there.

"That's it, lioness," I say, my orgasm so close that I can taste it. "Now, baby. Come for me *now.*"

And she does, tightening so hard that I swear I black out, or maybe that's because my orgasm is ripping through me, tearing my insides to shreds, leaving my knees shaking and my legs struggling to work and—

"Woof!"

It's muffled through glass.

But demanding enough to snap me out of my haze.

And same goes, apparently, for Ivy because she stills, laughter bubbling up in her, filling the air around us.

It's beautiful, that sound.

Almost as beautiful as the smile she tosses me over her shoulder. "Children," she says on a mock sigh.

Grinning, I pull out, help her get dressed, and we go inside to start the day.

But the more minutes that pass, the more I'm left with the certainty that this woman is worth the fear, the need, the pleasure, the joy.

That she's worth so much more than that.

She's worth the world.

My world.

And I'm determined to make sure she knows that.

CHAPTER THIRTY

Ivy

MY HEART IS POUNDING as I approach the conference room.

"You sure you don't want me to stay?" Knox asks quietly as I hesitate outside the closed door.

I inhale, hold it until I feel my nerves start to calm.

The call from the legal team about noon wasn't unexpected, especially considering that the story of Hiller being fired was already circulating in the media and on social media.

There was no explanation given—at least on the team's front —but that doesn't mean that rumors aren't already flying.

I have no doubt that some internet sleuth is going to figure it out and…

My temple throbs.

I hate it.

But I can't control it and…dammit, I did nothing wrong, so—

Fingers on my cheek. "I'll stay."

I exhale, clear my head. "I think I'd rather you distract Evie."

His eyes soften. "Does she know something's up?"

"I don't think so, but she's smart, and Haley is dropping her off in a few minutes, and if she sees me like this—"

He nods. "She'll suss something out."

"Yeah," I murmur.

"Then I'll go wait out front with her and distract her with the promise of Game Night and puppy time."

A new development, and one that seemed completely counterintuitive to everything that happened...and yet completely right.

Because if I'm going to stop hiding from my life, going to start going after what I want, what I need...

Then it's getting to do things like Game Night.

And getting to bring Evie along with me.

And—

Getting this over with, figuring out how to deal with the shit that's about to be heaped into my lap, or maybe processing the plan to move forward and knowing...

That I don't have to do this alone.

I nod. "Thanks."

He tugs at a strand of my hair. "No thanks needed, lioness." His eyes flick to the door. "And I know you can handle yourself, but if you need backup, just send me a text." Before I can tell him I'll be fine, he brushes his lips over mine. "See you soon."

And then he's walking away from me.

And I'm in the hall with bruises on my neck, my arms...and somehow feeling more safe than I've ever felt in my life.

With that thought, I knock on the door.

It's whipped open a moment later to reveal a full house— Coach Joey and Damon Connors and the legal team, including Tera, who helped me with my emails to the school district.

"Come on in, Ivy," Damon says, gesturing at the only open chair around the huge wooden table. "Please take a seat."

I want to pretend that I'm unaffected and assured as I move around the table, want to pretend that my heart's not pounding and that Knox is right about Damon, about my job being safe. I want to pretend that I don't care if he's wrong and they *do* fire me.

But it's all lies.

My knees shake as I walk.

My heart pounds.

My palms are sweaty.

Still, I know that I finally have people around me who'll help me pick up the pieces, and that gives me the strength to make it around the table, to settle into that open seat.

It happens to be next to Tera, and I glance over at her. "Thanks for your help with the letter," I say quietly.

"Any time," she replies, just as quietly. "Did it do the trick?"

I smile. "Yup."

She smiles back, mouth opening, but before she can speak again, Damon clears his throat.

And my heart starts pounding all over again.

"I'd like to first apologize on behalf of the team," he says, and I don't miss that his eyes are fixed on my throat, where the bruises are visible. "That never should have happened."

"No," I say. "It shouldn't have."

"You need to know that this will in no way affect your job," he says, "and if you'd like to leave we will fully pay out your contract and write you a letter of reference—"

I suck in a breath.

"And while we acknowledge that Travis Hiller was wrong in his actions, we don't acknowledge any wrongdoing by the organization as a whole."

Tera tenses next to me, and I see a flash of anger slide across Damon's face before I look to the man who chose to speak in his place.

The head of the legal department, Don Blackwell.

I bite my tongue as he continues, "It was an unfortunate series of events, and we've taken steps to prevent any further bad behavior by firing Hiller. We're also committed to a full investigation into his time here and will be hiring an outside firm to evaluate our working conditions and inclusivity, in order to make sure something like this doesn't happen again…"

Yeah, that's more like what I expected.

Dancing and prevaricating.

And, though I listen more about their plan to implement safety measures and the forthcoming investigation, I know it's not about me.

It's C.Y.A.

Cover your ass—or theirs, anyway.

"All right," Damon mutters several minutes later. "You gave your spiel, Don. Ivy understands what actions the team will be taking—" A pause, his eyes flicking in my direction.

I nod in agreement.

He nods back, goes on, "So now you all can take off and enjoy the rest of your Saturday while Ivy and I talk."

Don sputters. "I don't think—"

"Out," is all Damon says in response. "Everyone except Ivy and Joey."

There's a momentary pause, Don seeming to weigh arguing, but it's alleviated by Tera standing up and beginning to gather her things.

"You'll be okay," she murmurs as the rest of the table follows her actions, packing up and beginning to slip out of the room. "And if not"—she presses a card into my hand—"I'll make certain of it."

I swallow hard but nod again. "Thanks."

A squeeze of my shoulder and then she's snagging the folder from the table in front of her and following the others out.

Don is the last to go, as though he's fighting his every lawyerly instinct in leaving this room.

But he eventually *does* go, though he leaves the door open.

Damon sighs, crosses the room, and closes it.

"What else?"

My brows fly up. "What do you mean?"

"What else has happened between you and Hiller?"

Cold creeps into my veins, and my stomach begins to twist itself into knots. "I didn't— I never—"

His expression softens even as his hands clench into fists. "Forgive me," he whispers. "I didn't mean to insinuate that *you* did something."

"I—" I close my eyes, throat suddenly tight. Then open them again.

Joey pushes up from her chair, moves around the table and sits in Tera's chair. "What Damon means is that we both know it couldn't have been the first time he bothered you." Her voice is even, steady, and I'm thankful for that calm.

It means that I'm able to take several deep breaths, able to ease the ache in my throat, able to nod.

"It wasn't the first time," I say. "He's been harassing me from almost the moment I began working here."

Damon curses quietly.

"I told HR and that backfired—"

Another curse.

"How?" Joey asks.

"He was furious and threatened my job and..." I sigh. "I didn't have a fallback plan."

Damon jerks, rage on his face, but he stays silent and I turn back to Joey. "I should have told someone else—I know that I should have. But I have Evie to worry about, and..." I exhale. "He never went that far before."

Encroaching into my bubble and angry words and wandering hands became...

More.

"Will you tell Tera everything that happened?" Joey says.

My first instinct is to say no—nothing good comes from trying to make people like Hiller pay. It didn't do any good with my parents, with my boyfriends, with Evie's dad, how could it possibly make a difference now?

But...

This is different.

I have Knox—and Ella and Nova, Lake and Riggs and Leo and Storm. I have Damon and Tera and Joey.

I'm not alone.

And I *have* to show Evie that there's another way.

"I'll tell the detective who took my statement last night," I say quietly. "But Tera can be there to listen."

Respect in Joey's eyes, and she nods. "Okay."

"And your job?"

I glance over at Damon. "I'm not leaving."

Minus Hiller, I've loved working with the team—it's challenging and exciting and it pays well...and it means I get to spend time with Knox.

It's a no brainer.

"You don't have to decide today," he says. "The offer can stay on the table until you're ready to make a decision."

How had I thought this man cold?

Probably all the scowling.

But this conversation has told me enough—he's a teddy bear beneath the grumpy exterior.

"I'm staying."

He nods. "Okay, but if you change your mind..."

"Thanks."

He shrugs, turns back to his papers, as if he can't stand my gratitude.

Closed off.

Grumpy.

Hurt.

Yeah, I know something about that.

But I have a life to get to, a kid to parent, a man to appreciate.

The surly GM can't be my problem—not right now, anyway.

I push up to my feet. "If that's all"—I tilt my head to the door —"Evie will be here soon, and I want to get on with enjoying our Saturday."

In answer, he just inclines his head again, snatches the papers up, and walks out of the room.

Joey snorts. "Man's always got to make an exit."

My lips twitch as I turn to her. "Thanks for what you said."

"It's what needed to be said." Her hand covers mine for a moment. "But I want you to know that Damon and I both mean it—we have plans for the team, and none of them involve allowing this kind of bullshit to continue to run rampant. The organization has lost far too many good people because of the toxicity in the back office, and we intend to make sure it doesn't keep happening." She stands. "And, in case it's not clear, we know that you're good people, and we want you around, and you're doing excellent work for the team."

My eyes are stinging for a whole other reason.

Something she sees, I know, because the fierceness in her tone gentles. "I'll leave it alone," she says quietly. "But I won't leave *you* alone."

I blink up at her.

"Be prepared to be annoyed with my presence in the weight room."

My mouth quirks, and I start moving to the door.

"Well, then, I guess I'd better make *you* a workout plan too."

And as I walk into the hall, the boulder that had been sitting on my chest for far too long finally gone, I hear something wonderful.

Her laughter.

I'm smiling.

I'm moving forward.

And…I'm not alone.

Yeah, something wonderful is right.

CHAPTER THIRTY-ONE

Knox

THE NERVOUS ENERGY is almost palpable from the passenger's seat.

Same as the excitement flowing forward from the back of the car, Evie all but bouncing in her booster seat, Winter picking up on that feeling and eagerly staring out the car windows as we wind our way up to Lake's cabin.

Okay, it's less cabin and more expensive, luxury log home.

But the man came from money and models in his spare time —the face of watch brands and underwear alike. He's in another level of income than me, and I make good money as an established and successful player in the league.

"Woof!"

I glance at the back seat, see that Winter has recognized the house.

She and Steve have only met twice, and the interactions were watched closely—because she's still sporting her cast for a few more weeks—but the troublesome pup clearly made an impression on her.

I just hope her adoration doesn't turn into copying his behavior.

I don't need a demon dog on my hands.

Ivy exhales and I don't miss that it's shaky. Nervous, more so maybe than this afternoon's meeting. She shared what Damon said, what Joey said, what that asshole from the legal department said, and, more importantly, what *she* said.

And I'm so fucking proud of her.

But right now, I also want to throttle her.

She faced all of that—faced all the shit in her life—and she's scared of some snacks, cocktails, and getting into an argument over *Ticket to Ride*.

I shove that down as I park in front of Lake's place, but when she goes to hop out of the car, I snag her wrist, turn her to face me, and cup her jaw.

"Lioness," I say quietly.

"I'm fine," she says before I can go on.

"Yes, you are."

"I've been to Game Night before."

"Yes, you have."

But she hasn't been as *mine*.

"I'm fine," she says again.

My lips twitch and I lean over the console, kissing her, probably far more deeply than I should, considering that Evie's in the back seat, gathering up her stuff.

"Breathe," I whisper as I pull back. "And maybe consider that this is a chance to build that family you've always wanted."

"Woof!"

Evie pops her door and starts to get out. "Let's go, Mom!" A beat. "And Knox!"

I brush my lips over Ivy's one more time then rest my forehead against hers for a moment. "Let's go kick some ass in *Uno.*"

Finally, she relaxes enough to smile back at me. "I hope you're prepared to be skipped at least three times."

"Not four?"

"If the card gods allow me such a blessing then be prepared."

Grinning, I unbuckle and go to free Winter from her jail in the back seat then take Ivy's hand when we catch up with Evie, who's almost at the front door.

It swings open before we can knock, Nova appearing in the opening with a copper mug in one hand, the demon dog known as Steve tucked under her other arm, and a welcoming smile on her face.

But, just as quickly, she's pushed out of the way by Ella who holds up a hairbrush and a bottle of glitter spray. "Who's ready for a hair party?"

Evie squeals and runs inside.

Ivy takes the proffered mug, allows Nova to loop her now free arm through hers and draw her into the house.

Lake steps into the now vacant door, mouth quirking. "Beer or mule?"

I'm driving my girls so—

"Beer," I say as I step inside and put Winter down so she can say her proper hellos. By the time I'm done supervising her and Steve's reintroduction and accept the beer from Lake, I look up—

And the last bit of worry I was holding on to disappears.

Ella's braiding hair, Nova's dealing cards, and Jolie and Ivy bend over to scratch the pups when the meander their way over. Storm is concocting something in the kitchen, having put Riggs and Leo to work by chopping vegetables, if the knives and looks of extreme concentration are any indication.

God help us if anyone loses a finger.

"You okay?" Lake mutters.

I turn to him as I sip my beer. "Me?" I ask. "Or her?"

Ivy's wearing a turtleneck and I know it's part defense mechanism, part to cover the bruises so Evie doesn't look at them too closely.

She noticed them, of course she did, and while she accepted the vague answer that Ivy gave her, I know there will be more questions forthcoming.

The bruises are too obvious and Evie's too smart—emotionally and otherwise—and she cares about her mom too much to let that go forever.

"You," he says. "*And* her."

"I'm…" I sigh. "Not okay, exactly, because how can I possibly be after that happened to her?"

He nods.

"But she's safe and Hiller's gone now and…" I sigh. "In some ways it helped cut through the bullshit. I'm not going away, she's accepted that, and we talked last night and this morning, hashed some things out."

"I'm glad." He drops his voice. "I saw the release the team put out about Hiller in the media, and my agent asked me to prepare a statement just in case. Is that—" He cuts his gaze to the side. "Did that go okay?"

I shrug. "As well as can be expected. She had a meeting with Damon, Joey, and the legal team this afternoon." I fill him in on the details that Ivy shared with me. "Any other woman and I swear they'd be falling apart, but Ivy"—I shake my head—"she's rallied, is determined to keep working with the team, and swear to fuck was more scared about Game Night than the potential of facing Hiller again."

Because she's been through this before.

Because the look in her eyes last night tells me that she's been through worse.

"She's been to my place before," Lake says, his brows dragging together. "Did something happen—?"

"No. It's just that—" I trace my finger through the condensation on the outside of the bottle and sigh. "She's been through a lot, man. And she doesn't trust that she's not going to go through more, that she and Evie are not going to end up alone again."

Lake's silent for long enough that I glance back over at him.

And one look at his face soothes some of the edges of anger in me.

He's ready to commit murder on Ivy's behalf, and my woman needs more of that energy in her life.

"We'll make sure she knows that's not going to happen," he mutters.

Laughter echoes through the room and we both look toward the source of it—the women and Evie.

And I have total faith in him.

In *them.*

In the family I've made.

And the family that's going to become Ivy and Evie's too.

CHAPTER THIRTY-TWO

Ivy

"Oh, God!" I cry out and immediately clamp a hand over my mouth.

Knox growls, nips the inside of my thigh as water sluices down my skin. "You know that I love to hear you moan, lioness," he says against my pussy, the water and his words, his lips and teeth and tongue driving me insane. "But Evie's sleeping in the next room over."

Yes, she is.

Hence the hand-clamping.

But when his fingers join the party, thrusting into me and sending sparks of pleasure through my body, I know I'm still being too loud.

Hopefully, it's early enough that a knock won't be coming on the locked bathroom door.

He sucks hard at my clit and my hips buck.

And I figure it's got to be.

Or, more likely, that I won't be able to hear it, anyway.

"Come for me, lioness," he orders and my pussy spasms,

wanting to listen to him, desperate for the pleasure I know is sure to come.

Still, I shake my head.

Because I want something else more. "Together," I pant. "Inside me."

His smile is wicked, and he doesn't move, just drops his head and goes back to fucking me with his fingers and tongue.

I groan, my head falling back against the tile.

And there's no holding it back.

My orgasm tears through me.

He moves then, spinning me so I brace my hands against the wall, jerking my hips back so my ass is in the air.

I hear a crinkle, and then he moves closer and I feel the blunt head of his cock at my entrance.

"Yes," I whisper. "*Yes.*"

He groans as he presses into me, as he fills me, as he fucks me slow and deep and...

I jerk, my insides clenching around him, another orgasm so damned close I can taste it, can *feel* it, can—

It's here.

"Oh God," I pant, coming apart, pleasure spiraling through me, my knees giving way.

Knox doesn't miss a beat, just wraps his arm around my middle, holding me up as he continues to thrust—once, twice, three times.

"Fuck," he growls. "*Fuck*, lioness." He groans, strokes going uneven, cock pulsing, and body shaking as his climax hits him.

"You've killed me," I say when I can finally form words again, five minutes or five *hours* later.

He presses a kiss to my shoulder and slowly pulls out, sending aftershocks of pleasure all through me. "I've killed you?" he asks lightly. "*I'm* the one who's somehow supposed to play hockey tomorrow after this quad workout."

My lips twist and I brush my hand over one thick thigh. "I think these legs will hold up just fine." I grin when he helps me straighten and turns me to face him. "And trust me, I've put enough work into crafting these things, so I know."

He chuckles. *"You've* put the work in?"

"Yup," I say tartly, snagging my bottle of conditioner and going back to what I'd been doing before Knox invaded my shower...to greatly pleasurable results.

"Rude." He kisses the tip of my nose then steps out of the shower to take care of the condom as I finish washing my hair, massaging the conditioner into the ends, smoothing it up the length of the strands, keeping it off my scalp.

The shower door opens back up with a quiet *creak*, and then I get to enjoy the sexy show that's Knox.

He snags the loofa, adds enough soap to wash an elephant, suds it up, and starts smoothing it over his naked body, leaving tempting trails of white bubbles in its wake.

"Lioness."

I drag my gaze up from the hardening length of his dick. "Yeah?"

And yes, I sound extremely needy.

"I don't have time to fuck you again," he mutters, "so keep those sexy thoughts in your head."

"I didn't say them out loud," I point out, and dunk my head under the water to rinse out the conditioner.

He pinches my nipple, and I gasp, lids flying open.

Before water can get into my eyes, he's tugging me forward and out of the stream—which also has the pleasurable consequence of being pressed against his chest, our naked and soapy bodies rubbing together, sliding back and forth...

"Not helping," he growls.

"You started it," I remind him.

A nip to my bottom lip and then he's bringing us back into the stream, rinsing the soap off.

He's hard.

I'm wet.

But he meant it when he said he didn't have time for a round two—he needs to leave for a road trip and the bus to take him to the airport leaves far too soon.

I sigh. "I feel like we're just starting to figure things out, and you're leaving."

He stills.

"I know it's your job," I hurry to add. "And that it's a reality of your life, I just…"

He turns off the water, snagging a towel from where he hung it over the top of the shower's door—and I definitely mean *he* hung it because I always forget and have to get out naked and shiver my way over to the towel bar. He wraps it around me, big hands efficiently drying me off before he grabs the other towel and wraps it around his waist. "You just what?" he asks as he ushers me out.

My mouth kicks up and I sigh again. "I'm going to miss you."

His blue eyes…the warmth in them has my heart squeezing. "Thanks for saying that, baby." He touches my cheek. "And yeah, being on the road *is* part of my life, and it's going to be a lot less fun now knowing that I have you and Evie here waiting for me."

Another pulse of my heart, but before I have to find something to say—should I go with sweet because his words are sweet? Or sassy because he loves it when I'm sassy and I want him smiling and not sad when he has to leave?—he doesn't give me the chance to choose.

He just keeps talking.

Sigh. Adlers and their talking.

"And anyway," he says, "you'll have Evie and Ella along with Nova and Jolie to keep you busy."

I tug on my robe, leaning back against the counter and enjoying the show of him getting ready almost as much as I enjoy the truth of his words.

Game Night as his girlfriend was…

So much more than I could have dreamed of.

Saturday night, Ella and company welcomed us with open arms—not that they hadn't been willing to include us before—it was just...what happened with Hiller, their kindness afterward, the easy friendship offered at Lake and Nova's place—

It meant *more* because I was open to it, to them, to the possibility that Knox was right.

Evie and I don't have to be alone.

We can make our own family.

We can have that *more*.

"Plus, lioness," he says, brushing his lips over mine. "We'll do what the other guys do to stay in touch while the team's on the road."

"What do they do?" I ask. "Or should I say, what are *we* going to do?"

His lips quirk. "We'll text and call *and*"—he waggles his brows, making me laugh—"we'll have lots and lots of FaceTime sex."

I giggle and then by unspoken agreement we finish getting dressed. We tag team—he packs the last of his things into his suitcase, lets Winter out for her morning potty, and feeds the furry critters while I wake up Evie and get her ready so she can come with us to drop Knox at the rink, where the bus will pick the guys up.

Our kiss goodbye outside the bus generates more than a couple second looks, but not as many as I would have thought—probably because it's early, or maybe because Knox and I have circled around each other for so long that the guys figured something like this happening was inevitable.

Or maybe, I think, as Lake tugs the end of my ponytail before he gets onto the bus, a certain hockey captain is running interference for us.

Likely all three, if I have to hazard a guess.

And then it's time for Knox to leave.

He crouches in front of Evie, saying something to her that makes her smile, nod, and throw her arms around his neck. He hugs her back before straightening with her clinging to him like a little spider monkey.

"Just a couple days, lioness," he murmurs, brushing his mouth over mine one more time for good measure.

"Just a couple days," I agree.

One more kiss and then Evie's in my arms and he's getting onto the bus, waving at us through the window as the vehicle pulls away.

"Mom?" Evie asks, her gaze fixed on the road, where Knox and the team are disappearing from sight.

"Yeah, baby?"

"Is Knox going to be my new dad *now*?"

I still, those words ping-ponging through my insides. But, for once, I'm not afraid. "Is that something you would want?"

"Uh, yeah," she says, as though I just asked the dumbest question ever.

Grinning, I settle her on her feet. "Then yeah, honey bun. I just think he might be."

CHAPTER THIRTY-THREE

Knox

I JAB my finger in the direction of Riggs.

Then Lake.

Then Leo.

"You breathe a word of this to anyone..." I threaten.

"Dude," Lake mutters. "We're *all* a part of this. It gets out and we'll never live it down."

Leo nods his agreement.

"Yup," Riggs says, repositioning the laptop.

"Okay, now that the threatening is out of the way," Ella says, her voice slightly tinny as it plays through the speakers on the computer. "Can we get down to business?" She yawns. "It's late and I have Donna in the morning."

"*Cherié*, we can do this another time," Riggs interjects, looking ready to slam the computer shut and kick us all out of his room.

"Pish," she says. "How long can it possibly take to teach you guys this?"

"You might be surprised," Leo says dryly.

I glare at him, not needing his snark right now.

"Is there a reason no one has threatened *me* with silence?" Storm pipes up from the chair we've set up in front of the computer's camera.

"No," we all say in unison.

If there's one thing that we know about Storm, it's that he's loyal.

A good friend.

And someone who, once his trust has been earned, will keep our confidence, no matter the situation.

Case in point?

Since he's the only guy on the team with long hair, he's been called into service.

Yup. He's willingly sitting here with three of his teammates, my sister on video call, and surrounded by a plethora of hair paraphernalia that Leo picked up from the drugstore around the corner waiting to get his hair braided.

Yeah, if any of this gets out, we are so totally fucked.

"We all know," Ella says through the video call, "that you're a sweet little innocent baby."

Storm scowls at her. "I'm twenty-four."

"Like I said." She winks at him. "A baby."

His scowl deepens. "That's not exactly a—"

"Let's get on with this," Riggs interrupts. "God knows how long it will take, and Ella needs to get to bed."

"My bossy, grumpy hero," she trills, holding her folded hands against her chest and fluttering her eyelashes at the camera. "However did I live without you?"

"You didn't," Riggs says. "Not really."

The air tightens in the room, and I know that we're all feeling the same thing—

The utter truth in those words.

Well *all*, maybe, except for Storm, who glances over his shoulder at us and asks, "What?"

"Nothing," Lake mutters, lacing his fingers together and stretching them out in front of him. "Let's do this already."

Thankfully, if there's one thing that my sister is serious about (besides the people she loves), it's hair. "Right," she says, turning so her back is to the camera and lifting a comb. "The first thing you'll do is section the hair like this..."

I pick up the comb on this end of the video call, try to mirror her movements, and within five seconds of *sectioning* I know this is going to be a long ass night.

"Fuck," I say, grasping at the strands, trying to match my sister's movements and knowing I'm failing hopelessly.

Her sections are smooth, with even edges.

Mine are...

A mess of uneven lines and tangled hair and—

"Ow!" Storm cries.

"Jesus," Lake mutters.

"You'll want to be a little gentler," Ella says, turning to study me through the screen. "Kids generally have more delicate scalps than adults."

I freeze. "I could hurt her?"

My sister's face softens. "Knox, honey. A little tug on anyone's scalp"—she narrows her eyes at Storm, who's rubbing the side of his head—"won't truly hurt anyone."

Storm drops his hand. "Says who?"

Leo slugs him. "Dude. It's hair. Shut up."

"Okay, ready to go again?" Ella asks.

I nod, going gentler this time—because I won't hurt Evie, I fucking *won't*. As I make this attempt, I don't miss Lake, Leo, and Riggs leaning in, paying closer attention this time as Ella orders me to run the brush through Storm's hair and then goes through the sectioning again, this time even more slowly.

"Good," she says when I finally manage to separate Storm's hair into two relatively even portions. "Now, take the clip and use it to hold the half you're not working on out of the way."

It takes an unreasonably long time for me to accomplish that.

But I do.

"Good," she says again. "And now you're going to separate that section into three parts…"

After much cursing, many failed attempts, and Leo helping me hold one of the strands, I finish one braid, tilting my head to the side and studying my handiwork.

"It's not…" Rigg trails off, probably struggling to find something nice to say about the lumpy, uneven mess.

"Great?" Lake says.

"That bad," Leo says at the same time.

I glare at Lake, nod in approval at Leo.

"You'll get better the more you practice," Ella says. "Now, get going on the second half, yeah?"

Storm groans but dutifully holds still as I work through the second half, and my sister is right.

My second attempt is far better than the first, and I don't even need Leo's help.

"Good, hon," she says once I've finished and figured out how the tiny bows work—and yes, I'm very aware of how ridiculous the lot of us must look just now, Riggs and Lake debating the merits of the right choice of bow—bright pink vs multicolored vs extra super-duper glittery while Leo sits on the edge of the bed, stretching a random elastic on his fingers, out and in, out and in.

"Can I take them out now?" Storm grumbles.

I nod, see Leo surreptitiously snap a pic with his phone, and smother a smile.

Blackmail material.

I like it.

"Okay, boys," Ella says on another yawn. "Have fun playing dress up. I'm signing off."

I thank her, and Riggs snags the laptop to give her a more private goodbye as I start tugging out the bows and elastic, unraveling all of my hard work in far less time than it took in the first place.

Riggs tosses the closed laptop on the bed and starts shoving the hair stuff in a bag.

But when I've finished undoing the braids and Storm goes to stand up, Lake clamps a hand on his shoulder, pushing him back down into the chair. "My turn."

We all gape at him.

His mouth hitches up. "I need to know too."

That gaping doesn't subside.

"Nova's pregnant." His smile deepens because...*still* gaping. "And if we're having a girl then I need to know enough to pull my weight."

My eyebrows are at my hairline.

Leo's frozen like a statue.

Storm's eyes are wide.

Riggs unsticks first. "Congrats, man," he says, yanking Lake into a hug and pounding him on the back.

That gets us moving and then we're all hugging and exchanging our congratulations and...

Braiding each other's—cough, *Storm's*—hair.

It's a long way from a puck bunny in a hotel bar, but as I watch Lake struggle with the strands, contemplate bow placement, Leo and Riggs (and Storm) advising him in the process, I can't help but think...

It's a thousand times better.

CHAPTER THIRTY-FOUR

Ivy

ELLA'S EXPRESSION when she glances at something on her phone is cat-eat-the-canary, but she doesn't comment on it.

Just locks the screen and sets it face down on the table.

"Do I want to know?" Nova asks.

"Nope." Ella picks up her apple turnover. "I mean, maybe eventually, but until then…" She mimes locking her lips and throwing away the key.

Laughter bubbles up in my chest.

Nova sighs but clearly knows her friend well enough to not push the issue. She turns to me. "What time do you have to grab Evie?"

Not just *her* friend—Ella's mine too.

And Nova. And Jolie.

I have friends. I have more.

Evie and I…well, we're building that family, that place where we belong.

And all of us—minus Evie, who's at the aforementioned school—are chowing down on apple turnovers that are the size of our heads, though I did get the girls to pair the yummy treat with an equally yummy vanilla protein shake. Together, they taste like apple pie a la mode *and* they'll sustain us through lunchtime.

See?

Planning ahead.

Looking after them in my own special way, the same as they'd looked after me.

"She's going to Blake's house after school for…" I trail off, not finishing my sentence because—

"What is it?" Ella whispers, concern etched into her face as she reaches across the table and takes my hand.

I inhale and lift my chin. Then exhale my anger.

I need to be calm, steady. For Evie.

For *me*.

"The principal at Evie's school," I tell them.

Ella's anger isn't so easily dispersed. "The bitch who was trying to suspend her?"

I nod, clench my back teeth together because maybe my furious Mom Rage isn't so easily displaced either. But calm. Steady. A breath and then I deliberate slap a neutral smile on my face. "Oh, hello Ms. Hearst," I say pleasantly as she pauses by our table.

Her beady, snake-like eyes narrow. "Are you happy with yourself?"

My mouth drops open, eyebrows shooting up, and I don't know where the hell my next words come from, except to say that I've been hanging around Ella a fair amount of late and that rage…it burns *deep* enough to unlock my inner snarky bitch. "I mean, I always say that there's room for improvement, but yeah" —I shrug—"I think I'm doing pretty well."

Nova chokes.

Ella's fingers spasm around mine.

Jolie glances down at the table, but not before I see the smirk on her face.

Ms. Hearst's eyes widen, then narrow again. "Excuse me?"

I just hold her stare. "You heard what I said."

"Care to join us for a coffee?" Nova offers. I'm not sure if she's trying to diffuse the tension or attempting to get Ms. Hearst to realize that she interrupting so she'll go away.

One look at the coolness in Nova's green eyes and...yeah, it's the second.

I sip my protein shake. "She probably has to get back to doing her job."

Ms. Hearst gasps. "How dare you?"

The genuine outrage has me freezing, setting the bottle back down, and frowning. She's far more upset than I'd expect, even given our last interaction.

She glares at me. "I can't believe you have the gall to say that after what you did."

"What *I* did?" I ask, my confusion giving way to anger again. "*You're* the one who tried to suspend my daughter."

"And because of that, you saw fit to get me fired?"

I freeze, my eyes going wide. Because, I mean, I wouldn't mind getting her fired, but also...I hadn't, unless—

"Yeah," she snaps. "Exactly."

And she starts to storm off.

"I didn't—"

She turns back.

I lift my chin. "I didn't do anything except tell the truth to the people who cared to make a difference." I hold her eyes. "It's not me who didn't do my job."

"Those parents—" She clamps her teeth together.

"What?" I ask. "Make more money than me? Had more pull —or so you thought? Would make more of a fuss than me?" I place my hands on the table and push up to my feet. "Well, you were wrong. I trusted my daughter to your care, and you returned her to me bruised and scared, and wanted to punish her for it! Of course, I was pissed! Of course, I did everything I could to keep her safe!" I exhale. "But I didn't get you fired.

That's on the school district. That's on the superintendent. That's on *you*."

She glares at me. "It's not fair."

"Neither is punishing an innocent child."

Her chin lifts. "All these parents are so damned entitled these days, sticking their noses in where they don't belong, thinking they know better—"

"Right. Well, if anyone thinks they're entitled then it's certainly not me." I drop back into my seat, turn away from her.

She sputters. "I—"

Ella leans forward. "In case you missed it…that's your cue to leave."

"I—"

"Bye," Jolie says, joining me in turning her back on Ms. Hearst.

My heart is pounding, and my hands are shaking, but I did it.

Said what I needed to say in this moment. Stood up for myself. For Evie. And then ended it on my terms.

Yeah, I fucking did it.

Ms. Hearst lets out an outraged sigh, but thankfully, storms off.

"That. Was. *Awesome!*" Nova says once she's gone, bumping her shoulder against mine.

Jolie salutes me with her protein shake and a smile.

"Maybe I'm a dick"—I shrug—"but I'm happy she was fired."

"Not a dick," Ella says. "And I imagine you're not going to be the only one who's happy she's gone."

"No, I'm not," I agree, filling them in on some of the things other parents had confided in me, what Brian, the superintendent, had told me, and the emails Tera from the legal department had helped me draft.

Nova's eyebrows are at her hairline. "That's…"

"A lot," Jolie finishes.

"It is," I say, rubbing the spot just above my heart, where a knot I didn't realize I still had has just loosened. *"Was."*

"Yes, *was.*" Ella takes my hand, voice gentling. "You did amazing."

"Thanks, Ells." I grin. "Thanks to all of you."

"You did good, kid," Nova says.

"Definitely," Jolie agrees. "That was prime snark and I'm here for it."

"Oh, you are so totally stuck with us now," Ella says, grinning wide.

"I had help," I say. Help I accepted, and for the first time in my life, hadn't been burned for. Help I could trust. "Because they definitely don't want double the Adlers storming the school's office as my backup."

Ella winks. "We *are* dangerous."

"Dangerously *annoying*," Nova teases.

"No," Ella says. *"Dangerously annoying* would be mentioning that you haven't touched your apple turnover, which is unusual for a lot of reasons…" Her mouth twitches. "But paired with the fact that you also haven't been partaking in any of our delicious mule combinations—not even your favorite, honey rosemary combo—I would be very *dangerously annoying* to mention the pieces I've put together."

Jolie's eyes are wide as they lock with mine, her words slow. "Is she saying what I think she's saying?"

Nova scowls at Ella. "You're unbelievable, you know that right?"

"Unbelievably hilarious, smart, and beautiful?" she asks, fluttering her lashes. "Why yes, I do know that."

I chuckle.

Nova jabs a finger at me. "Don't encourage her."

I take a page out of Ella's book and mime zipping my lips.

"All of this is your fault, you know."

I lift my eyebrows in question.

Her nose wrinkles. "You fell for an Adler and thus encouraged this sort of behavior."

I give up on the zipped lips and unleash my secret weapon— or at least what I noticed when I first arrived. "*I'm* not the one hiding the baby-themed gift at my feet."

Her mouth drops open.

Jolie cracks up.

I shrug. "Just because I don't talk as much as an Adler"— though there are times where I really, *really* enjoy the talking, like, say, when Knox is murmuring naughty things in my ear— "doesn't mean I'm not sneaky like one."

For some reason that has Ella grinning.

But before I can ask what that smile with more than a dash of wicked is all about, Nova bends over, snags the bag, and thrusts it to Ella. "I was going to ask you to be a godmother, you brat," she snaps.

All humor leaves Ella's face and I don't miss the way her eyes immediately tear up. "Really?" she breathes.

"Yeah. Who else?" But then Nova softens too, swiping away a tear that slides down Ella's cheek. "You've been there for me forever, Ells."

Jolie takes my hand, squeezing tight, and I'm thankful for the contact as they hug, their words becoming so quiet they're inaudible. But it's impossible to not feel the sentiment behind them—and *that's* enough to make my eyes burn and tears clog up the back of my throat.

I sniff.

Jolie sniffs.

Nova and Ella are already lost to tears.

But even amongst all the damp eyes, it's the happiness in the air that soothes my soul.

And maybe also, it's the apple turnovers.

CHAPTER THIRTY-FIVE

Knox

I LOVE HOCKEY.

Fucking *love* it.

But I can honestly say that this is the first time in my life that I've been itching for it to be over so I can go back home.

Can go back to Ivy, to Evie, to Winter and Snowball.

Texts and calls aren't enough.

Sexy, naked FaceTime isn't enough.

Ivy was right—leaving right when we started figuring things out blows.

And it doesn't help that everything with Hiller exploded while we were gone—swear to fuck, if I have to dance around one more question about the bastard, I'll track him down myself, show him exactly what it feels like to be covered in bruises.

Not today, though.

Today, I'm going to see my girls.

> KNOX: Hey, lioness. We just landed. I know it's getting near Evie's bedtime, so I can take an Uber to your place if you want.

The sun is setting in the distance, but I can't wait till tomorrow to see them.

I *can't*.

But even though that antsy energy is flowing through my limbs, I resist the urge to text again. It's Monday and they'll just be getting home from karate. Then there's dinner to be made, homework to do, furry critters to take care of.

Her response comes after we've loaded up onto the bus that'll take us back to the rink where mostly everyone's car is.

> IVY: I think you should go to your place—

No lie, my heart convulses at those words.

Luckily, I'm a fast reader, so it's only for a moment.

Because then I see the rest of the text.

And my heart pulses for a completely different reason.

> IVY: Evie and I caught the Plague. I want to see you, but we've been down with fevers (and worse) all night and I don't want you to get sick.

> IVY: I know we drove you, so you don't have your car, but do you think someone can give you a lift home?

There's a lot to unpack in that, but I just focus on what's most important.

> KNOX: Rest, my lioness. One of the guys can bring me back.

> IVY: Thanks, Knox. I'm sorry.

> KNOX: No apologies, baby. I'll see you soon.

> IVY: I'll give you the all-clear when we won't contaminate you.

Heart twisting, I swipe out of the text chain. "What's that look for?"

I glance over at Lake as I start typing on my phone—only this time it's not to message my woman. "Think you can give me a ride to Ivy's?"

His eyes narrow. "What's wrong?"

"She and Evie are sick."

"That sucks."

"So?" I say as we pull into the lot, hitting the button to submit the order for soup and simple sandwiches for dinner, and then promptly opening a different app so I can get Sick Day groceries and supplies.

My captain claps me on the shoulder. "Consider Lake Jordan's Taxi Service at your disposal."

I pause and turn to him as the bus pulls to a stop and he starts gathering his stuff. "Lake?"

He lifts his eyebrows in question.

"I've seen it, you know," I say quietly. "What you've done for me, for Ivy, for Evie."

He's run interference, made sure her part in Hiller's demise stayed between the small group of us and not the assholes on the roster. And further that, he's made it clear that he approves of Ivy and I together—and that anyone talking shit is going to have to deal with him.

In short, he's given us space.

In short, he's been a good friend.

A good *brother.*

He starts to shake his head, but I stop him.

"I see it," I say, clapping him on the shoulder and holding his stare. "And I appreciate it."

He stills. Then his big chest expands and collapses on a slow, deep breath. "You had a hand in bringing me Nova." His eyes warm just at the sound of her name. "The least I can do is make sure that you have the same."

"Except you always have to one-up me." I mock scowl.

"Do I even want to know?" he asks dryly.

"You gave me two for the price of one—Evie *and* Ivy." I grin.

A shake of his head.

One I ignore because I go back to my grocery order.

But I don't miss that he's grinning too.

———

I KNOCK on Ivy's front door, knowing I'm doing the right thing, but nervous all the same.

What if I mess this up?

What if I don't give her what she needs?

What if—

The door swings open and—

All of those worries disappear in a flash, certainty settling in their place.

Yeah, I'm *absolutely* doing the right thing.

Holy hell.

She looks like death warmed over—pale skin, dark circles beneath her eyes, hair in a knotted ponytail that's barely clinging to life.

"Knox?" she asks, and I wince.

Her voice is a rasp, and my throat convulses in sympathy.

"I thought I told you—"

I brush my knuckles along her cheek, then lightly grip her shoulder and guide her back inside. "Hush now, lioness," I say, shutting the door behind us. "When's the last time you sat down?"

A shake of her head, her eyes distant, her ponytail giving up its fight and collapsing.

"Evie woke up in the middle of the night not feeling good and then the puking started." She shudders. "So much puke. I need to finish cleaning—" She takes a step toward the kitchen and nearly falls over.

"Right," I mutter, shooting out a hand, steadying her, and

when she wavers again almost immediately, I curse softly and scoop her up into my arms.

"Wh—"

"You need to be in bed."

"But the dishes— And Evie—"

"I got it, baby."

"You don't have—"

"Lioness." I wait until her bleary eyes meet mine. "Remember what I said before?"

"You're not leaving?" she rasps.

"Exactly." I kiss the top of her head, feel the heat just blazing off her and start carrying her down the hall, not stopping until I'm in her room and settling her on her bed. She's shivering and pale, but her color's high.

Definitely spiking a fever.

"Medicine?" I ask quietly.

She winces, rubs her temple, like that's too loud, but says, "Gave Evie her dose a couple hours ago."

"And you?" I murmur.

"I—" She just shakes her head. "I don't remember."

Of course not. Which means that she and I are going to have a talk later—after she's feeling better—about her taking better care of herself.

Or, at least, allowing me to do it for her.

"Stay here," I order softly then go into her bathroom. The medicine's on the counter, so I snag the proper dose then dampen a wash cloth. The latter goes on her forehead, the former I set on the bedside table.

Water. Maybe some crackers to soothe her stomach before she takes it.

"I'll be right back," I whisper.

"I can—"

I tuck the blankets a little more tightly around her then slip out to the kitchen...just as there's a knock at the door and the groceries are dropped off.

"Perfect." I retrieve the bags, head into the kitchen, and put the necessary items away, taking note of the dishes and pile of laundry on the table. *Later.* I fill a cup with water, grab some crackers and a few other things for Ivy. On the way back to her room I pop my head in to check on Evie and find her sleeping.

Then I'm back in Ivy's room, setting the packet of crackers, water, and cup of flat Sprite next to the medicine on the side table.

"Knox?" she rasps.

I tuck an arm behind her, coax her to sitting. "See if you can keep this down, lioness."

She nods weakly but manages to nibble at the cracker I pass her then to take a few sips of the soda.

"Now the medicine, baby."

She gets it down, but I don't miss that even sitting up this long takes it out of her.

"Just relax. I've got you and Evie."

"You don't—"

"I know I don't have to," I tell her, flipping the towel so the cool side is against her skin. "But I'm not going anywhere, lioness, so stop asking."

Her eyes fix on mine and there's the strength, the steel in her —even if it's just a flicker making it through all that sick. "I was going to say," she whispers, "that you don't have to be here, but thank you for it anyway."

"Oh," I mutter.

The barest flicker of a smile. "Yeah. *Oh.*"

Grinning at her tartness even as something inside me settles, I help her lie back and smooth down her hair.

"What did you give me?" she asks, her lids heavy.

"Cold medicine," I tell her. "And Mama Adler's famous sick day protocol."

Her brows drag together. "What's that?"

"Flat Sprite and saltines." I touch her flushed cheek. "Cures even the most stubborn stomach."

"Knox," she whispers, her hand finding mine.

"What?"

"Your mom." Her fingers squeeze mine. "I'm sorry you lost her."

"She's alive in here"—I touch the spot above my heart—"and here"—my temple—"so even though she's not in this house, fussing over you and Evie like it's her job, she gave me the tools so *I* can."

"*Knox.*"

"What's up, lioness?"

"I'm not sure I know how to handle this," she murmurs.

"You're not used to people being kind to you." I lean in and kiss the top of her head. "But that's going to change, baby. I'm going to make sure of it."

"Men," she whispers.

"What?"

"I'm not used to *men* being kind to me." She turns her palm over, lacing our fingers together. "With men it's always been rough hands and sharp words and forced—" She breaks off.

Forced.

Christ.

It takes everything in me to not yank my hand from hers and then go and plow it into the wall, over and over again.

"That time is done," I say instead.

"I know," she murmurs, "because you're my safe place."

"Dammit, lioness."

Confusion in pretty brown eyes. "What?"

I touch her cheek. "I really want to kiss you for saying that."

Her mouth curves. "Do it later when I don't have the plague."

I chuckle. "Exactly."

"Is Evie—?"

"Sleeping."

Relief sliding across her face.

"Thank you."

"I'll let you rest." I start to push up from the bed but her fingers catch mine. "Need something else, my lioness?"

"Yeah."

I flip the towel on her forehead again. "What's that?"

Her eyes are hazy, but her words are clear. "Will you stay a little while and tell me?"

"Tell you what?"

"About your mom."

I still, heart squeezing, understanding exactly how much courage it took her to make that request. Deepening our connection. Allowing me in. Knowing every part of me.

It feels big.

As big as her letting me hold her after Hiller hurt her.

As big as...her opening her heart to the potential of us.

So it's not even a question as I settle back down on the edge of the mattress and smile, picking out one of my favorite memories. "Well, there is a funny story that involves Ella, me, our dog Max, and a jar of peanut butter."

She giggles. "Tell me more."

I do, and I'm just getting to the part where my mom returned home to find Ella, myself, and Max covered in peanut butter when I look down and see her eyes are starting to slide closed.

Bending, I brush the backs of my knuckles along her cheek. "Rest now, lioness."

"But I need to know how it ends," she whines quietly.

"You will." I stand. "Because I'll be around to tell you."

CHAPTER THIRTY-SIX

Ivy

I VAGUELY REMEMBER LISTENING to a story about a jar of peanut butter, a very happy dog, and Knox and Ella furiously scrubbing their kitchen before their mom came home.

I vividly remember dreams—of being so dizzy I could barely think straight while changing sheets and cleaning up puke; of that night with Hiller, hands squeezing too hard, my words not penetrating his drunken haze; of Evie's sperm donor and the night he'd hurt me, the night that finally made me realize nothing would change and I needed leave; of being sent house to house to house as a kid, never feeling like I belonged.

Okay, so maybe they're memories, nightmares, things I want to forget.

I struggle to shove them away, to swim out from beneath the swirling memories—

Soft hands touching my cheek, coaxing me up.

"Drink this, lioness," I hear.

Even with the dark memories curling through my mind—those unwelcome hands—I recognize the voice that speaks and don't panic.

Then there's a cup pressed to my lips, and I peel open my eyes enough to see Knox, to remember where I am and what's happening. "Evie?" I rasp.

"Fine," he says quietly. "Actually better than fine. She's feeling herself again."

Relief slides over me. "I'll—"

"You'll rest, baby," he says. "*After* you drink this and take your medicine, okay?"

I don't have the strength to argue, just eat the cracker and sip from the cup he holds up then swallow down the medicine with a shudder. "My throat hurts."

"I know." A gentle touch coaxing me to lie back. "I'm sorry, lioness. Try to sleep—you'll feel better when you wake up."

Words bubble up in the back of my throat.

There's something I want to say, something I *need* to say.

Only the moment my head hits the pillow they poof away like so much smoke.

Dreams descend...

But this time they're not nightmares.

They're bright spots of sunshine on a cold, winter day— Evie smiling as she breaks a board in karate; Knox working his ass off in the weight room; colorful pictures on my fridge; Evie and me watching a Sierra game, cheering as Knox scores; Game Night with Ella, Nova, Lake, and the rest— battling through *Uno*, kicking butt in *Ticket to Ride*, losing terribly in *Abducktion* but not caring because Knox's happiness is enveloping me; noshing on delicious apple turnovers with Ella, Jolie, and Nova last week, never feeling out of place.

And I sleep, knowing that Knox is right...

I can have this.

I can have so much more.

I can *love* him.

My mind clears, peace filling me, and I sleep the sleep of the truly exhausted.

———

THE NEXT TIME I ROUSE, I feel slightly better, and the medicine goes down easier.

"Knox," I whisper, those memories still floating around in my mind, but some part of me needing to touch him.

He kisses my temple, takes my hand. "Rest, baby."

"I—" I frown, the words slipping out of grasp.

"It'll hold, lioness," he whispers. "You can tell me later."

Since I'm too exhausted to do anything else, I allow my eyes to close and sleep to take me under.

And I do so, the happy memories fill my mind again.

So, I sleep and sleep and *sleep*.

———

THE NEXT TIME I wake up, it's to find Evie in bed next to me, watching her tablet.

Ella's perched at the end of the mattress and her head swivels my direction the moment I try to sit up.

"Easy," she murmurs, rounding the bed and slipping her arm beneath my shoulders. "Let me help you." She tucks a pillow behind my back and passes me a cup. "Just water," she says. "Knox is making a grocery run."

A blip of guilt slides through me, but I shove it down.

"Thanks," I rasp, my throat still feeling like the fires of hell, though at least my head is mostly clear. "What time is it?"

"Eleven in the morning." A beat. "On Wednesday."

My eyebrows fly up. "I've been out of it for two days?"

Ella's mouth kicks up. "Afraid so." Then she touches my forehead. "Nova's in the kitchen, whipping us up a treat. Do you feel up to real food?"

My stomach rebels and regretfully, I shake my head. "No, I don't think so."

"So the Mama Adler special then?" She holds up the packet of saltines.

I nod. "I think that's for the best."

She passes a couple over to me. "I'll get the Sprite."

"Thanks, Ells."

She smiles. "You're family, Ivy. No thanks needed."

My heart pulses, but I tuck those words close, right with the happy memories.

When she's gone, I turn to my daughter. "Doing okay, baby girl?"

"Yup," she says, and I can't lie. It's exceedingly nice to not be on my own right now. One look at Evie and I know she's entered The Zone—the one that every mom dreads. She's feeling better while I still feel like hell, and she's been cooped up for days without school, without friends or dance or extracurriculars. The tablet is only going to keep her entertained for so long, and then she'll be raring to go.

While I just want to curl up in a ball and cry.

But Ella's here. And Nova.

And Knox is getting groceries.

My...family.

My heart skips a beat, even as the truth of that settles deep. Because, yeah, that's what it's supposed to be.

"Is your voice raspy because of the bruises?" Evie asks.

I still, hand coming up to my throat. The bruises have long healed. But my daughter has a long memory. "I...Honey..."

Her eyes fix on mine, and I know that I owe her the truth—or some form of it anyway.

"My throat's sore from being sick, baby. The bruises are gone"—I pull my sweatshirt down—"and not to blame. You said your throat hurt too remember?"

A slow nod. "Yeah. But my voice didn't sound like that."

"That's true." My lips curve. "But I didn't puke as much as you did. Remember?"

She nods again.

"Sometimes when people get sick, they feel bad in different ways."

"Oh."

I inhale.

Exhale.

And know I need to give her a little more about what happened. Because if she's still thinking about it after all this time...it's bothering her. I push down the blip of guilt, worrying her and—

I don't want my baby girl worrying.

"I know I told you I got hurt at work," I say, weighing my words carefully, struggling to find the right ones to give her the truth without scaring her. "That's true, but the full story is that someone there wasn't very nice to me and tried to hurt me."

Her eyes go wide.

Dammit.

But I press on.

"Kind of how James wasn't nice to you, remember?"

Her fingers press lightly to the skin at the top of her cheek, where the black eye had extended. "I remember," she whispers.

"And just like with James, things got worse before they got better."

"Did Knox make it better too?"

Like he had with Ms. Hearst.

"Yeah, baby. He helped make it better. And like you did," I add, needing to remind myself that I wasn't just victim as much as I need her to remember her *own* courage, "I stood up for myself too, and now I don't have to deal with the bully anymore."

Her eyes hold mine, staring intently, clearly searching for the truth.

Then she pivots in typical kid fashion.

"'Kay," she says, and then, with all the aplomb of an elementary-aged kiddo, she moves right along, her focus returning to her tablet and the video playing on the screen.

But I'm not quite ready to let my baby go back to the brain rot, especially since I've been in and out of it for two freaking days. "Ella did a great job on your braids, honey."

She deigns to glance at me. "Ella didn't do them."

"Oh," I say, "I didn't realize that Nova could braid."

A shake of her head, the bows clipped to ends of her hair bouncing. "Nova didn't do them either."

My brows drag together and maybe I'm hazier than I realize. But nope, her hair has been carefully corralled into two neat braids that are hanging down her back *and* secured with bows that match her pjs.

Um.

Maybe she's been bingeing YouTube videos and has gotten more skilled than me? Or Jolie came by for a bit? After all, she's a hairstylist at the same salon that Ella works at. Or—

Evie looks up again. "Knox did them after I took a shower," she says before flopping back onto the pillow, her focus returning to her video.

My mouth opens. Closes.

Knox did them?

Knox?

But it's not surprise that slides through me, not really, once I think about it.

Because *of course* he had fixed Evie's hair, same as he fixed the situation at school, with Hiller, with The Plague.

With my heart.

I open my mouth again, not even sure what I want to ask—

"He asked me to teach him a few weeks back," I hear from the door, seeing Ella standing there with a bowl in one hand and a can of Sprite in the other. She walks toward me, her eyes as warm as her smile. "Said he'd need to know." A beat. "For the future."

My pulse speeds.

My mind races.

But...there's no fear, no knot in my stomach, telling me that this will eventually go wrong.

Instead, my soul is happy.

My heart is full.

And the truth is bound to every cell.

"Of course he did," I say softly.

Because that's the man he is.

Because that's the man I *love*.

I remember the words coming in my sleep, feeling them in my heart, my soul, but *thinking* them while I'm conscious? Not something I would have allowed even two days ago.

Right now? With all this beautiful truth surrounding me?

How can I not?

Because my love for him isn't anything like what I've experienced before. And it's nothing like what I used to think the emotion was. It certainly isn't anything like what the people who hurt me in the past once held over me. Nor is it me desperately seeking any sliver of affection or kindness, no matter the cost. This a pure love, a *safe* love, a love that doesn't hurt or wound or burn.

It's braids for my daughter. A cool washcloth for my head.

Kind words. Listening hard. Food and dishes, texts and hugs.

Game Nights and sandwiches and taking care of us when we're sick.

It's making our own family, our own peace, our own future.

It's *us*.

And somehow, because of all that, it's not scary in the least.

But, also, somehow, *because of all that*, I know that I need to find the perfect way to tell him.

"Ells," I begin. "I'm wondering if you might—"

"Yes."

I blink. "You don't even know what I'm going to ask."

A delicate shrug. "Doesn't matter," she says. "The answer's still yes."

"Thank—"

"Nope." She shakes her head. "And there'll be none of that either. I meant what I said the other day—you're stuck with us. Just like I meant what I said this morning—no thanks is needed"

Family. Love. Safe.

Slip. Slip. *Slide.*

Or maybe… Slip. Slip. *Stuck* is more apropos.

My lips curve and Ella smiles back before she passes over the Sprite—stirred flat, exactly as what I've learned the Mama Adler Special calls for.

I sip and turn back to Evie, studying the even strands of her braid, the perfectly matched bows.

And I shake my head.

"How is it that everyone is better at braids than I am?"

CHAPTER THIRTY-SEVEN

Knox

I'M UNPACKING the bags of groceries and starting to put them away when Ella sweeps into the kitchen with Evie.

"My little Evie needs more glitter," she announces, snagging her purse from the counter and slinging it over her shoulder. "Ivy's sleeping."

"Uh..."

But I don't get the chance to finish that because just as abruptly as they'd come into the kitchen, they both bustle from the room.

More glitter—yeah, right. I've seen Ivy's craft cupboard. There's no possible way Evie could need more glitter.

Still, I don't bother arguing.

My sister is a force amongst giants; if she's declared that Evie's getting glitter then Evie's getting glitter.

Shaking my head and smiling, I listen to them gather their stuff and head out the front door. I move down the hall, lock up behind them, and then finish putting the groceries away.

Sometimes it's just better to let the ladies do their thing.

Smirking, I shove the reusable bags into each other then do what I've been itching to do from the moment I left her—

I walk down the hall to Ivy's room.

I have a game tonight, so I'll need to head out soon for the rink.

Before then, though, I need my Ivy fix.

Only she's not in bed when I push the door open and slip into her room.

Frowning, but figuring she's probably using the toilet, I sit on the edge of the mattress and wait.

And wait some more.

Worry twisting my insides, I move to the bathroom and cautiously poke my head in. She's sitting on the counter, staring at me as though she's been waiting for exactly this.

"Um…" I begin, heart suddenly in my throat.

"Knox," she says, hopping off and moving toward me.

"You okay, lioness?" I ask, getting my shit together and meeting her halfway. She's pale, her eyes a little wild, but instead of stepping into my outstretched arms like I expect, she shifts and steps by me, going to the door—

Slam!

"Um," I say again, spinning to face her, that worry transforming into a tornado. "Ella took Evie to get some glitter from the craft store."

Ivy stills, dropping her head against the door. "Heaven help me. *More* glitter?"

"Kind of what I said, but nothing was going to stop those two." I chuckle, expecting her to turn toward me, to show me that beautiful face and laugh along with me at the intractability of the dynamic duo. When she doesn't, I go back to frowning. "Um, baby, are you going to look at me?"

"I—" She shifts, grunting as she messes with something.

"Ivy," I say, my patience giving way. "What the hell is going on?"

"Noth"—another grunt—"*ing*. I'm—" There's a groan, a *crunch*. "This seemed a lot easier the other time," she mutters, her shoulders shaking, her body straining and—

Creak!

"There," she sighs, finally spinning to face me with…

The door knob in her hand.

"Um…" I know, I know, it seems to be a reoccurring theme for me today, but…

What the actual fuck is going on?

"Right," she says, with a chagrined smile. "This seemed so much easier in my head."

I take the knob from her hand, look from it to the door and back to her. "Are you going to clue me into *what* you thought would be easier?"

Her mouth ticks up. "Breaking that." Her smile fades. "Saying this."

My heart sinks.

And that worry explodes out of me in the form of word vomit.

"Lioness, I know that things are moving quickly, but if you need us to slow them down, need me to back off a bit, I can—"

I mean, I won't, because I'm fucking addicted and I love her and need to claim her as mine, forever, but I can move at her pace, can do whatever I need to do in order to make sure she's comfortable and safe, to make certain that Evie's equally as safe and as comfortable.

"No," she says, settling her hand on my chest, above where my heart is pounding. "It's not that."

My brows drag together. "Then what is it, lioness? Is it about me sleeping over? I know Evie has probably asked questions, but I made it clear to her when you were out of it, that I was just sleeping on the couch while you need some extra help—"

Her hand moves, lifting, and she presses a finger to my lips. "It's not that either."

"The job?" I ask, peeling that finger free. "Working together creating a conflict of interest?"

She shakes her head, whispers, "No. Not that either."

"My traveling?" I touch her cheek. "I know it's a drag. But I also get to be home a lot—"

"No."

"Is it—"

"I love you!"

I freeze, every cell in my body going still, my heart spasming, my pulse skittering, my knees going a little weak. "What did you say?" I rasp.

Her shoulders rise and fall on a breath, and then her head comes up, eyes locking with mine.

The air in my lungs freezes.

There's no fear in her beautiful brown eyes, no panic or reservation. Just...*love.*

"Lioness."

Her mouth kicks up. "You Adlers talk so much, I knew that when I realized how I feel about you"—she settles her hand on my chest again—"when I realized how deeply my emotions for you are, I *knew.*"

"Knew what, lioness?" I cover her hand with my own.

"Knew I had to beat you to the punch and tell you that I love you first."

"Dammit, baby."

She grins. "I know." Her fingers flex against me, the barest bite of her nails on my flesh.

"Why the door knob?" I ask.

"Ella and I were brainstorming ideas," she says, her cheeks going pink. "She asked me when the first time I realized we were going to be more was, and it..." Those cheeks go even redder. "It was, well, when we were stuck in the weight room and..."

"The sparks between us could have set the world on fire?"

"Yes," she whispers. *"That."*

"Fuck, I love you."

She gasps. "You do?"

"Was there any doubt?"

Stilling, she tilts her head to the side, as though considering that, but it's that beautiful mischief that sets my heart pounding. "No," she says, "I suppose not."

"That's my girl." I brush my knuckles along her cheek. "So, who's going to spring us from bathroom jail if Evie and Ella are at the store?"

"We'll just call them, and they'll come home—" She drops her hand, steps back, and pats her pockets.

"What?" I ask when she freezes and she looks up at me in horror.

"I left my phone on the nightstand."

"That's okay," I say, reaching for my own pockets. "I have —" But I still too, realizing that I left my wallet and phone in the kitchen. Cursing softly, I refocus. "We'll put the knob back on."

She winces. "I think I broke it. I was trying to loosen the screws and"—she grabs the knob, holds it up—"well, I kind of got nervous, gave it up, and…" She nibbles at her bottom lip. "I broke it."

I take it from her, examine the bent metal. "Yeah, baby, I think you fucked it."

Another wince. "I'm sorry. I know you have to go to the rink."

"Not for a while yet." I toss the knob to the side, wrap an arm around her and yank her against my chest. "And don't be sorry." I slip my hand beneath her shirt, run my fingers along her bare skin. "I can think of *plenty* of ways to pass the time."

"Oh really?" she asks, and I feel a hundred feet tall when I see the light in her eyes, the mischief, the *love*.

"Yup," I murmur, drawing her closer, lowering my head—

Right as the door bursts open and Ella and Evie hurry in.

"Did you tell him?!" Evie exclaims, hopping from foot to foot. "Did you tell him?

Ivy grins, presses her hand to that spot on my chest, just over my heart. "Yeah, baby, I did."

She stills. "And did he say it back?"

Those fingers flex, but I answer for Ivy.

"Yeah, short stuff, I sure did." I jerk my head toward us. "And if you come here, I'll tell you too."

Evie's expression...

It's fucking beautiful.

And then she's running toward us, throwing her arms around our middles. "This is the best day ever!"

"Is it because you got Ella to buy you more glitter?" Ivy asks dryly.

"Yup!" Evie's arms tighten around us. "But also because we finally have a family!"

"You've always had a family, Evs," I tell her, scooping her up and holding her tight. "Now I'm just lucky enough to be a part of it."

She hugs me, then wraps her free arm around Ivy's shoulders. "Knox *is* going to be my new dad."

"I sure am, short stuff," I say. "So long as that's what you want."

She nods so energetically she looks like a bobblehead.

I chuckle, tug one of the braids I made that morning. "Then that's what you get."

Another hug, this one so tight that she's almost choking me.

"I love you, Evs," I murmur.

And just like her mom, the look in her eyes...well, it's the best gift on the planet.

Or maybe that's actually the words she gives me next.

"I love you too, Knox."

Ivy's free hand finds mine, squeezing hard.

I squeeze back, heart hurting in the best way, but before I can say anything else there's a sniff from behind us.

Ivy hears it too because she turns to my sister and lifts an arm. "Want to get in on this family group hug action, Ells?"

My sister doesn't hesitate, just wraps her arms around us and joins in, and for the first time since my mom died, I know—

I'm not my dad.

I'm not my job.

I'm not the possibility of what *might* happen.

I'm *me*.

And that's just what they need.

Which means it's just what *I* need.

EPILOGUE

Ivy, One Month Later

THE KNOCK at the front door has me frowning as I close the computer and glance at the clock above the microwave.

It's too soon for Evie and Knox to be home, the former at dance and the latter watching Evie dancing her heart out as she learns her new tap routine.

Dinner is simmering on the stove—a simple vegetable soup that I've paired with some chicken breasts. We'll have hot chocolate for dessert because Nova's finally taught me all of her secrets and Evie and I are thoroughly addicted.

And speaking of Nova, she and Lake are down in the Bay Area, scouting out locations for their wedding.

Their *shotgun* wedding.

I grin as the knock comes again.

Ella then, stopping by because she's bored.

Maybe with Jolie, who does my neighbor's hair, apparently, and is the reason the guys and Ella sussed out that things were heating up with Knox and me.

Not that I mind the nosiness—nor the gossip, since I know it comes from a good place.

From love and concern and…

Those dang Adlers wanting to be involved in everything.

Knock. Knock. Knock!

"Right," I whisper. "Focus."

I turn for the front door, making a pitstop to turn down the soup, and hurry down the hall, whipping the wooden panel open.

My first mistake was not looking through the sidelight to see who's standing on my porch.

The second is not slamming the door immediately in Travis Hiller's face.

Instead, my mouth drops open and my fingers spasm on the wood and I *don't* move.

Which leaves time for *him* to move.

He steps forward, hand outstretched and—

"You little bitch," he growls. "Do you know what you've done to me?"

I snap out of my shock, shove his hand away. "Don't touch me!"

He stills for a moment, probably shocked that I'm not just standing here, letting him do what he wants to me.

But I've learned.

I've grown.

I've found my place and fuck all if I'm going to let this asshole ruin it.

"Do you understand what you've ruined?" he growls, stepping close enough that I can smell the liquor on his breath.

Something inside me *snaps.*

Maybe my control.

Maybe my temper.

Maybe all of that pent-up female rage.

"Do you understand what *you* did to *me?*" I take a step toward him and his eyes go wide.

Yeah, definitely that pent-up female rage is making an appearance.

"All my life the men in my life have hurt me," I growl, moving forward as he skitters back a step. "*All* my life they have abused and yelled and made me feel like I'm not valuable, not worthy of respect and love."

"I—"

"But know what?" I take another step toward him, watch with no little amount of satisfaction as he stumbles down the porch stairs. "You are just the latest in a long line of assholes."

"Well, you're—"

"And you know what *else* I've learned?"

I don't give him the chance to answer, just close the distance between us and shove him.

Hard.

He's drunk and angry, but he is absolutely no match for my St. Patrick's Day decorations—

Including my leprechaun-themed gnome.

With a sparkling green bow tie, and a sparkling orange beard, and a pot of—yup, you guessed it—sparkling gold...*gold.*

He catches his heel on the gnome, slips on a patch of last-season ice and—

Slams into the driveway.

"Woof!"

My temper fades in an instant and I whip around to see Snowball and Winter running through the door. I manage to snatch Snowball as she tries to run by me, but Winter scoots under my arm and hauls ass toward Hiller.

She growls and leaps at him.

"Ow!" he yells, reaching for Winter.

Who yelps.

I snap into motion, but not before...

I stop, skidding on that patch of ice and Evie appears out of nowhere.

She sprints toward Hiller, her flowy tutu flying behind her like a cape. "Don't you hurt Winter!" she yells, kicking him in the side hard enough to make him grunt and release Winter.

"And don't you hurt my mom!" she yells even louder as she scoops up the pooch and kicks him again.

Hiller's eyes flash and true fear slides through me.

But even as I reach them, Knox is already there.

"Please give me a reason," he says quietly.

But like most bullies when presented with someone stronger than them, Hiller wilts like a two-week-old rose.

He lifts his hands. "I don't want any trouble."

"Right," Knox mutters dryly as he reaches into his pocket and pulls out his phone.

When Hiller realizes who he's calling—the police—he tries to get up.

Knox just plants a boot into the center of his chest. "Stay," he growls before his eyes flick to mine.

I nod. "I'm okay."

His stare drags over me, head to toe then back up in careful examination. He nods slightly when our eyes meet again, as though silently agreeing with that statement. "Take everyone inside?" he says gently.

I nod again then bustle Evie and the critters inside, a good thing considering that Snowball is scratching the crap out of me.

By the time I get them into the house—and reassure Evie, giving her a hug and telling her how proud I am of her (and also to please—freaking *please*—never put herself in that position again), several cop cars have pulled up out front.

"Stay here," I order.

"Aw, Mom!" Evie complains.

Do I bribe her with an ice cream sandwich because I know it'll keep her busy and seated and *inside*? I sure as hell do. But I'm just as intent on finding out what's happening as she is, and desperate parenting times call for desperate measures.

I slip outside and Knox is immediately breaking off from the police officer he's speaking to, crossing to me and cupping my face in his hands. "You're really okay?"

"I didn't freeze." A shake of my head. "Well, I did. But only for a moment. Then I—" I cover his hands with my own. "I stood up for myself."

The barest sliver of amusement slides through his eyes. "I saw him eat shit on the driveway. That was your doing?"

"Yeah."

He shifts, tucking a strand of hair behind my ear.

"And Evie—"

That lightness in his eyes flits away. "I'm sorry, lioness. I told her to stay in the car, but she sprinted out of there so fast that I couldn't stop her."

"Aw, honey." I step closer. "You know she's an unstoppable force like all of you Adlers."

"She's mine," he growls. "*You're* mine."

Not missing that he's trembling, I press closer. "Yes, we are. We're yours and we're fine. Everyone's fine."

"You're moving in with me."

My heart skips a beat.

But I don't argue.

"Okay."

"I have a security system and I'm in the gated community. He can't get to you and—"

"Knox, honey, I said okay."

He freezes. "O-okay?"

I settle my hand on his chest, feel his heart pounding beneath it. "I love you. We're a family. And I'm tired of living in two houses." My mouth tips up. "Plus, you have more storage for glitter."

His exhale is shaky, and when he rests his forehead against mine, I don't miss that he's still trembling.

"Think Evie will be okay with it?"

And I know if I say no, he'll drop the entire conversation.

Because he loves me, loves Evie, and wants what's best for us.

"I think she will absolutely love to decorate another room with as much pink and glitter as she can muster."

He shudders but finally smiles a real smile. "I'll buy stock in sunglasses today."

I chuckle.

He runs the backs of his knuckles over my cheek. "Winter's okay too?"

"Yeah. She and Snowball are both fine—and I'm buying them both some serious treats for wanting to stick up for me."

"Damn right *we* are."

God, I love this man.

"Mr. and Mrs. Adler?"

My heart leaps again as we turn to the police officer.

Not because the assumption is terrifying…

But because it sounds right.

And, as we go over to make our statements, I know I now have another thing to plot with Ella.

Because I'm going to put a ring on it.

And I'm going to do it soon.

———

Joey

I'm sitting in my office and wondering how in the fuck I got here.

I mean, I *know* how I got the head coaching job for the Sierra —same as I know that part of me will never be satisfied with how it was bestowed upon me.

I didn't earn it.

Not wholly.

I'm the consolation prize, the diversity hire.

Or, at least, that's what the sports bloggers are saying.

Sighing, I settle back in my chair—or what has officially become my chair over the last days—and try to get my head together.

Tonight is my official first game as the head coach of the Sierra.

And I'm the first woman to ever get here.

And I need to make it count.

And I—

There's a perfunctory knock before the door opens and...

My lungs hitch.

Damon walks in.

Tall, grumpy, sexy as hell, and built like a male model, the man is temptation personified.

I've wanted him from the first moment I laid eyes on him.

Which was approximately one second before I came to terms with the fact that I could never have him.

Not just because he's my boss—

But also because he's untouchable.

The fallen hero who's clawed his way from the shadows back into the light. The avenging...not angel, because he's far from that, but the antihero with a savior complex and a moral code that's known only to him.

He's everything I lust after.

In fact, he's so perfect for me that it's like the universe peeped into my Kindle reading history and rendered a man from between the pages.

"You good?" he asks quietly, stepping close enough for me to see the scar crisscrossing his right eyebrow, the flecks of gold in his blue eyes.

I grab my tablet, loaded with everything I can possibly need to coach effectively tonight, and stand. "I'm good," I say as I move to the door—which, invariably, brings me closer to him.

His spicy male scent in my nose.

The heat that radiates from his body scorching my skin.

Those intent eyes fixed on me.

My fingers go limp and I drop the tablet.

"Joey," he mutters, bending with me, reaching for the tablet before I can grab it. He lifts it, presses it into my hands. "You're going to be fine."

"I know I am," I lie.

Because I *have* to lie.

I have the job. The weight of female representation already sits on my shoulders.

And the arena's full of fans—I can already hear the sounds of the crowd, even from our position in the depths of the arena.

I straighten then lift my chin, turn to go.

But the moment I reach for the handle, he's in front of me, those blue eyes blazing. "You know I wouldn't have hired you if I didn't think you were up for it."

I *don't* know that.

I mean, I *do*.

But I don't and—

"Joey," he says, settling his hands on my shoulders, crouching a little to hold my gaze. "You're up for this."

My heart—it can't take this.

Grumpy, bordering on the edge of asshole Damon, I can deal with.

Sexy, brooding, taciturn Damon, I can handle.

But sweet Damon with the encouraging words?

Nope.

This isn't good at all.

As if it wasn't bad enough that I was in lust with him...in this moment, I fall a little in love with him.

And I know he sees it.

Because he steps back as if he's been burned.

"Joey."

It's a cold rebuke.

"I need to get on the ice," I mutter, shoving by him, reaching for the handle. My fingers close around the cool metal when his words reach my ears.

"This can't be, you know that."

I turn the knob. "I know that."

"For a hundred reasons."

Gee, thanks.

"I know that too," I say aloud, pulling the door open.

"It *can't* be."

I glance at him over my shoulder. "Damon," I say quietly. "I'm well aware of every obstacle that stands in my way"—I hold his stare—"including you—"

He opens his mouth but I don't let him speak.

"—so just shut the fuck up and let me do my job."

Blue eyes spark with fury, kissable lips press flat, his ever-present frown deepens.

"Joey," he begins.

I do the only sensible thing I can—

I walk away.

But when I glance back at him before I turn the corner...

The look on his face has me falling even deeper.

———

Thank you for reading Knox and Ivy's! These two—and Evie hold a special place in my heart, so I hope you enjoyed! And check out the next book in the Sierra Hockey series, ON THE FLY. **He's grumpy and untouchable...until he falls for me.**

CLICK HERE TO READ ON THE FLY NOW>

———

And do you want a sneak peek into my BRAND NEW hockey series?

If you love big, bearded hockey players who fall hard and fast for the women they love, pick up book one in the Grizzlies Hockey series, MARRIED TO NUMBER TWENTY-TWO. **I signed the contract. I just didn't expect her to show up ten years later, ready to cash it in.**

. . .

CLICK HERE TO READ MARRIED TO NUMBER TWENTY-TWO NOW>

READ on for a sneak peek below!

Aiden

I wake up to a heavy knock on my condo's front door and glare blearily at my phone in the charger.

"Two in the fucking morning," I mutter, grabbing a pillow and clamping it over my ears. "It's two o'clock in the morning on my fucking birthday, and I have to deal with this shit."

This shit being my neighbors.

It's not the first time they've pounded drunk on my door, desperate for their roommate to let them in to what they think is their apartment.

This was sort of funny the first time.

I remember those days, drinking too much, being dumb.

But after the second and the third—where I gained status into the inner circle and a code to the keypad to their apartment door —it was no longer cute.

Now, six months later and countless times of bailing them out, I'm *so* not in the mood.

Especially when it's my fucking birthday.

The knocking cuts off and I think—*pray*—that they've gotten the hint.

But it's approximately two seconds later when it starts up again.

I glance at my phone again, see that really five minutes have passed, making it two-seventeen and officially my birthday.

Some present.

I could try to ignore it—but that just means extending the

torture. Sighing, I toss back the blankets and stomp to my apartment door, whipping it open to reveal a slender brunette on my doorstep.

"Ho, mama," she says, gaze taking a slow perusal down my body.

"Who the fuck are you?"

"It's me. Luna."

I stare at her, uncomprehendingly.

"From Rockfield?" she adds.

Recognition begins to dawn. "Luna Maybelle?"

"Yup! That's me." She nods, grinning, and I see it then, the glimpse of my best friend from the childhood rink I grew up playing at come out in her smile. Mischief and life. Joy and hard work.

Summers spent spending every spare moment together—her figure skating, me playing hockey.

But she's not little Luna anymore.

Christ, she's anything but—tall, beautiful, curves for days—and she's staring at me.

Because I'm staring at her.

Fucking hell.

I spur myself into motion.

"Luna! Oh my God!" I pull her into a hug. "What the hell are you doing here?"

"It's your birthday!" She holds up a piece of paper that looks faintly familiar. "And, well, it's mine too, remember?"

That's right.

We have the same birthday.

"We're both twenty-five, single, and—"

My eyes narrow in on the paper. It's crumpled and stained, as though it's years old.

A purple and pink swirl decorates the edges and suddenly I remember her painstakingly drawing it as we sat side-by-side at one of the high top tables of the ice rink, waiting for the Zamboni to finish cutting the ice.

Her brow had been furrowed. Her movements carefully controlled.

And I had been obsessing over how pink her lips were and what her butt looked like in her skating dress, so much so that I barely remember what we'd been drawing.

No, I think hard, grabbing on to those memories, not what we'd been *drawing*.

The contract we'd put together.

The contract my hormonal twelve-year-old self had signed.

With a sparkly pink colored pencil.

A giant boulder settles in my stomach, but before I can snap myself out of the horror of those memories, she shoves the paper in my hands then throws her arms around my neck.

"We're getting married!"

CLICK HERE TO READ MARRIED TO NUMBER TWENTY-TWO NOW>

SIERRA HOCKEY

Hate missing Elise's new releases? Love contests, exclusive excerpts and giveaways?
Then signup for Elise's newsletter here!

www.elisefaber.com/newsletter

———

And join Elise's fan group, the Fabinators (https://www.facebook.com/groups/fabinators) for insider information, sneak peaks at new releases, and fun freebies! Hope to see you there!

———

If you enjoy my series, considering supporting me on PATREON! Get access to early releases, bonus content, character art, audiobooks, special edition covers, swag, and much more!

CLICK HERE TO SUPPORT ME>

———

I so appreciate your help in spreading the word about my books, including sharing with friends! Please leave a review on your favorite book site!

ALSO BY ELISE FABER

Gold Hockey (all stand alone)

Blocked

Backhand

Boarding

Benched

Breakaway

Breakout

Checked

Coasting

Centered

Charging

Caged

Crashed

A Gold Christmas

Cycled

Caught

Cap

Covered

Crushed

Changed

Scored

Breakers Hockey (all stand alone)

Broken

Boldly

Breathless

Ballsy

Bewitched

Blowout

Breathe

Blazed

Sierra Hockey Series

Over the Line

Caught from Behind

The Big Skate

On the Fly

Rush Hockey Trilogy #1

Big Puck Energy

Filthy Puckboy

So Pucking Over It

Rush Hockey Trilogy #2

Love, Pucks, and Other Stories

All's Fair in Pucks and War

No Pucks Lost Between Us

Rush Hockey Novellas

Puck and Make Up

Eagles Hockey Series (all stand alone)

Broken Laces

Lace 'em Up

Knotted Laces

Loaded Laces

Lucky Laces

Billionaire's Club (**all stand alone**)

Bad Night Stand

Bad Breakup

Bad Husband

Bad Hookup

Bad Divorce

Bad Fiancé

Bad Boyfriend

Bad Blind Date

Bad Wedding

Bad Engagement

Bad Bridesmaid

Bad Swipe

Bad Girlfriend

Bad Best Friend

Bad Rebound

Bad Romance

Bad Business

Bad Billionaire's Quickies

Love, Action, Camera (all stand alone)

Dotted Line

Action Shot

Close-Up

End Scene

Meet Cute

Love After Midnight (**all stand alone**)

Rum And Notes

Virgin Daiquiri

On The Rocks

Sex On The Seats

Life Sucks Series

Train Wreck

Hot Mess

Dumpster Fire

Clusterf*@k

FUBAR

Perfect Storm

Free Fall

Lost Cause

Roosevelt Ranch Series **(all stand alone, series complete)**

Disaster at Roosevelt Ranch

Heartbreak at Roosevelt Ranch

Collision at Roosevelt Ranch

Regret at Roosevelt Ranch

Desire at Roosevelt Ranch

Phoenix Series **(read in order)**

Phoenix Rising

Dark Phoenix

Phoenix Freed

Phoenix: LexTal Chronicles **(rereleasing soon, stand alone, Phoenix world)**

From Ashes

In Flames

To Smoke

KTS Series (all stand alone, series complete)

Riding The Edge

Crossing The Line

Leveling The Field

Scorching The Earth

Cocky Heroes World

Tattooed Troublemaker

ABOUT THE AUTHOR

USA Today bestselling author, Elise Faber, loves chocolate, Star Wars, Harry Potter, and hockey (the order depending on the day and how well her team -- the Sharks! -- are playing). She and her husband also play as much hockey as they can squeeze into their schedules, so much so that their typical date night is spent on the ice. Elise is the mom to two exuberant boys and lives in Northern California. Connect with her in her Facebook group, the Fabinators or find more information about her books at www.elisefaber.com.

f facebook.com/elisefaberauthor

a amazon.com/author/elisefaber

BB bookbub.com/profile/elise-faber

O instagram.com/elisefaber

d tiktok.com/@elisefaberauthor

g goodreads.com/elisefaber